SADDLE WISE

2

THE
QUARTER
HORSE
FOAL

Inda
Schaenen

RP KIDS

PHILADELPHIA · LONDON

Dedication

*This story is dedicated to the memory of Chet, a blind,
sure-footed bay gelding, who carried my mom through the
Canadian Rockies in the summer of 1956.*

Library of Congress Control Number: 2008933254

ISBN 978-0-7624-3353-7

Cover and interior design by Frances J. Soo Ping Chow
Icons illustrated by Rich Kelly
Edited by Kelli Chipponeri
Typography: Affair and Berthold Baskerville

Published by Running Press Kids,
an imprint of Running Press Book Publishers
2300 Chestnut Street
Philadelphia, PA 19103-4371

Visit us on the web!
www.runningpress.com

chapter

Poor Hannah. As I swirled the currycomb and brush in two big loops across her warm shoulder, one hand following the other, I could feel the heat rise off the mare's glossy brown coat. Thick veins throbbed along her rear leg, and her stomach bulged as if there were a piano stuck inside her. Two big horseflies kept trying to land on her haunches. When a third actually landed on my arm, I smacked it with the brush so hard that the tough bristles left red marks.

Hannah shook her head, twitched the skin up and down her back to rid herself of two flies, and stomped her left front hoof an inch from the tip of my boot. I had been grooming Hannah long enough to know that this was her way of telling me she had just about had it with this whole thing—summer, standing still, and, for the last ten months or so, carrying a growing foal.

"It won't be that much longer, girl," I said quietly, thankful that all I had on was a tissue-thin tank top, old green cargoes, and work boots. "This heat must feel like a sauna to you."

Hannah's udder had been swollen for a few weeks, but today when I looked her over more carefully, I noticed drops of whitish milk. I would have to ask Mr. McCann what that might mean.

I heard a quiet nicker from the fence. It was Rainy Day, my own horse. He was a chestnut with a diamond-shaped white markings on his forehead, three white socks, and a pink scar across the left side of his jaw and around his eye. I peered into the shade of a black thorn tree where Rainy Day stood watching me.

We had been riding over to the McCann place for a couple of weeks now so I could help Mr. McCann with his farm chores while he recovered from a broken hip. Mr. McCann lived alone in a dilapidated house just outside Plattsburgh. His wife had died a few years back and his kids were grown up and gone. Earlier that spring, I had met him during the May floods, not too long after the truck accident that had scarred Rainy Day's face and put him in my life for good. Mr. McCann was the kind of old man people called crotchety, and at first I had been a little afraid of him. Eventually, after I had spent more time helping out around his house and his barn, I got to know him well enough to stop worrying about his crabby reaction to everything.

Rainy Day and I both loved riding out to his place. He

lived a few miles outside of town on a dirt road, which meant I could bring Rainy Day to a canter without worrying about cars and traffic lights. Sprawling green tree branches formed a shady tunnel over Boone's Passage, and different kinds of wildflowers bloomed along the roadside. As spring turned to summer, the colors and shapes of the flowers shifted, the lacy white blooms going to seed as the yellow black-eyed Susans began to flower.

Usually Rainy Day and Hannah hung out together in the pasture while I worked around the house and in the barn. Sometimes they trotted around side by side. Other times they stood nose to hip and hip to nose, swishing their tails and rubbing their chins across each other's backs. Either way, they acted as if they had a lot to catch up on. When I was done with the daily chores—feeding the pig, gathering eggs, tending the goat, shoveling out stalls, refilling water buckets—I whistled for Hannah to come over. She knew exactly what was in store and hardly ever made me come out to drag her back.

The sun hung low behind the barn and lean-to, where I was trying to clean the bits of leaves and dirt from her hair and make her coat nice and smooth for the night. Hannah neighed loudly. Even though the brushing felt good, she needed to announce to the whole farm how maddening it was to stand still for so long. Hannah was fifteen years old, and I was still relatively new at the horse-care business. No doubt the quarter horse mare thought I could be grooming her a little more efficiently. If I hadn't had her halter hooked to a rail, she would definitely have turned to give me the eye.

"Sorry, babe," I said quietly, "we're almost done. Hang in there."

Plattsburgh can be pretty hot in July, and this month was no exception. People complained about the weather no matter what the season, but they saved the worst of their complaints for summertime, when the temperature rose above ninety on most days and the humidity rose to rain forest percentages. It was the kind of muggy air that slammed you the second you left any air-conditioned place—your house, the grocery store, or the mall. "It's like an oven out here," was what people usually said, but I always felt like that was only half right. You weren't simply in an oven. You were trapped in a covered stew pot inside the oven.

I was brushing out Hannah's black bangs when I smelled cigarette smoke. That was the other thing about the combination of heat and humidity—smells were always more intense and traveled farther on seemingly no wind at all. "Ugh, Hannah," I said as it dawned on me what was going on. I put the brush down in the grooming box. "I'll be right back. This'll just take a sec."

I ran toward the house and went straight in the back door, past the kitchen, through the living room, and on out to the front porch. It was just as I suspected.

"Mr. McCann! Hey!"

"April Helmbach," he said, more grouchy than ever. "Am I paying you to do chores or to act as a private eye?" The burning cigarette was wedged between two thick fingers of his right hand.

"I'm sorry, Mr. McCann, but don't you want to get better?"

"I'm healing a hip, missy. My lungs are fine the way they are, thank you very much."

"Come on, Mr. McCann, you know that's not true," I pointed out, ignoring his tone.

"So now you're a physician?" he asked. "I should be calling you Doc Helmbach, the thirteen-year-old genius of the medical world?"

What a pain in the neck an old man could be! The trick with Mr. McCann was not to take his cracks personally. Sometimes it seemed like he was joking, other times like he wasn't. I once asked my Aunt Patti about it, and she said I was right to be patient with Mr. McCann's manner and to give him the benefit of the doubt.

"He's had his share of troubles and he's been alone awhile now," Aunt Patti said. "Plus, he grew up in a time when people weren't especially sensitive about how their words came out and who might get hurt by them."

"He's not politically correct, in other words," I said.

"Precisely," Aunt Patti said. "I don't mean to say there are no definite rules, because there are, but..."

"But?" I urged Aunt Patti to complete her sentence. She knew I hated it when she let a comment trickle off into nothing because she had decided it wasn't something I should hear. "But?" I repeated.

"But sometimes there aren't."

"So you're saying that sometimes there are no definite rules," I said, double-checking.

"I guess that's what I'm saying," she said, smiling. "But only sometimes."

I looked straight at Mr. McCann. His thin white hair lay scraggly over the top of his big head, and there was a whitish stubble in place of a beard. He had long yellow teeth and thin lips. His dirty old blue work shirt was only half tucked inside his brown pants, and he wore ancient-looking work boots whose laces he never tied. His cigarette continued to burn in his knobby hand. He was sitting in the plain wooden chair he used for his physical therapy. I could see the stained and crumpled copies of the exercise instructions on the wobbly wrought-iron table next to him.

Finally he looked up, and I spoke right into his watery gray eyes.

"Mr. McCann, I'm not a private eye, and I'm not a doctor. I'm just a kid who knows that smoking is bad for anyone and everyone. And one of the things it's bad for is circulation. And you need to have good circulation to heal a broken bone. With all due respect, sir," I concluded, a little sarcastically.

He laughed aloud, so I rallied my courage to say more.

"Besides," I said, "you're supposed to be doing therapy now, aren't you? The stretches and leg lifts and whatever."

"April! I swear and affirm that you are worse than that Cheryl what's-her-name, the one who comes over here once a week to torture me with these infernal contortions."

He leaned over and dropped his cigarette on the porch, then mashed it under his boot. I gathered up the crumpled sheets and set them in order.

"Don't you want to get better, Mr. McCann? I mean, it's bad enough you're not keeping up with your exercises, but smoking on top of everything?"

He actually smiled at that, as if I had told a joke. I didn't understand what was funny.

"My dear, I'm doing the best I can. Old geezers like me don't have the get-up-and-go about these things that you might. This hip will heal and I'll be all right again, or it won't heal and I will not be all right again. What will be will be."

"Well, I think you're being self-destructive and I don't understand it. If I were you—"

"Ah, but you're not me, are you?" He patted me on the arm.

"I'm almost done with Hannah," I said, putting the exercise pages in his free hand. "By the time I get done, you need to be done with these, too. See? I can be just as ornery as you, Mr. McCann. No offense."

Before he could respond, I skittered down the porch steps and dashed back around the house. I ran through the mown grass to Rainy Day. For a while he had seemed content hanging out in the pasture, plucking up tender shoots of clover and munching. But as I approached, he stamped one front leg impatiently and shook his head. I hugged him around his neck and kept my head there for a moment or two. In the six weeks since Rainy Day showed up in my life I had gotten better at figuring out what he was feeling at any given moment. Of course he couldn't speak to me in words, but by paying attention to the way he looked, and the ways he moved different parts of his body, I could tell whether he was afraid, angry, nervous, bored, or happy. I pressed my cheek against his long warm neck and I closed my eyes. "Are you too hot to hang around here anymore, boy? Ready to go home?"

He traced big figure eights with his head, which seemed like a "no." But if he didn't want to leave, why was he acting so fidgety? I looked up and saw that Hannah stood calmly watching us from near the barn, her tail constantly swishing at flies.

"Just a couple more minutes, Rainy Day, and we'll get going. Promise." I rubbed his nose and jogged back to Hannah.

"Sorry for the interruption, girl," I said. "Your old man is one stubborn dude."

After undoing her halter I gave her a good long rub along her stretched and swollen side. Could a whole new horse actually be in there? It seemed impossible. Then I felt something jab against my hand from inside Hannah. At first it freaked me out, but I quickly realized that it must be the foal kicking. How dare I doubt his presence, he seemed to be saying. *Jab! Jab!*

Well, I thought, patting along the wiry brown hide, at least someone at the McCann place was working their legs!

chapter

At dinner that night I complained to Aunt Patti about Mr. McCann. Lowell, my friend from next door, who was also in my grade at school, happened to be over. Lowell spent a lot of time at our house.

"I just don't understand it," I said. "Everybody knows how stupid smoking is, and he just doesn't seem to care. And why doesn't he take his therapy seriously? How is he ever going to be independent again if he can't use his legs properly?"

Aunt Patti was slicing me another piece of cold flank steak. She forked me a flat strip of meat. I spooned out another dollop of mustard and started cutting a bite.

"I don't know," she said. "Maybe deep down he's tired of being independent. Maybe he actually likes the company and likes having someone else do all his work for a change. Especially a cool kid like you. I bet you brighten his day."

Lowell snickered. "Yeah, April, just like you brighten my day," he said.

"Shut up, Lowell," I said. Aunt Patti could be corny to

the extreme, but I didn't feel like hearing Lowell's mockery just then. I watched as he snuck a piece of meat under the table to our dog Chase. The only person who ever fed Chase like that was Lowell.

Aunt Patti took another sip of soda. I had been living with Aunt Patti ever since I was four years old. She was my father's younger sister and had come to live with me when my parents died. Everyone in Plattsburgh knew the story, so I didn't have to repeat it often. My parents used to own a stable, Ozark Pastures, where they trained and lodged horses. One day they were working with a young filly. My mom was on her back and my dad was by her head when the filly accidentally stepped into a yellow jacket nest. The horse reared, threw my mom, and stomped on my dad's leg, instantly severing my dad's femoral artery. My mom came down hard on the ground and snapped her neck. The whole thing was a matter of a few terrible seconds. Everyone always said it was a fluke, as if that somehow made it more understandable or bearable. But it never seemed understandable or bearable to me. From that moment on, I had hated horses with my heart and soul. As far as I was concerned, a horse had killed my parents.

Years went by before another fluke changed my life again. This time it was a highway accident. Rainy Day had been packed in a transport trailer along with forty-one other horses. All of them had been sold off at auction to a horsemeat processor who was shipping them out of state for slaughter. The driver lost control of the truck and smashed across the center rail, and seventeen of the horses died. Others were terribly wounded. Aunt Patti and I happened to be heading into St. Louis not too far behind the accident and we got out of the car to see what had happened. It was during all this confusion that Rainy Day came wandering up to me. He had survived the accident but had blood streaming down his face and a deep cut on his shoulder. I still don't know what happened, but those few minutes we spent together staring at each other in the pouring rain changed me completely. I had banished myself from the world of horses, but ever since May, I was like a person returned from exile. Rainy Day helped me forgive his entire species. Within a couple of weeks, we had adopted him. Nobody was more amazed or relieved than Aunt Patti.

It wasn't like Aunt Patti was the mother I never had or anything. Sure, we looked a lot alike, with our curly dark brown hair and what Aunt Patti described as "our small but muscley physique." But we were definitely aunt and niece, not mother and daughter. I had friends who fought night and day with their mothers. Sometimes I told myself that I was relieved not to have to go through those constant battles. Aunt Patti and I were totally simpatico. Maybe because she seemed so young, I trusted her completely. I felt like she was always on my side, even when we disagreed. She seemed to see things from my perspective. We were like teammates: I went to school, and she ran her flower shop, Room for Blooms. Aunt Patti loved plants and insects. Before she came to live with me, she was going to be a biology teacher.

Right now Aunt Patti was making excuses for why Mr. McCann was refusing to follow his treatment plan.

"But why can't he do both?" I said. "Be glad to have me around *and* do the exercises he's supposed to do?"

"Old habits die hard," Lowell said.

Lowell had recently quit what everyone was sure was a computer addiction. His parents had been having a rough time for a couple of years, and Lowell disappeared into cyberspace. Right around when I adopted Rainy Day, Lowell turned his life around. His father got a better job, and he started exercising and eating right. Our having made what everyone called "a dramatic rescue" during the flood probably boosted his self-esteem.

Aunt Patti nodded.

"Smoking is an old habit," she said. "So is not exercising. A man used to hard physical labor on a farm will not have such an easy time switching to leg lifts and ankle rotations. It must seem stupid and boring to him, don't you think?"

"I guess," I replied, unconvinced.

"You want some more steak, Lowell?" Aunt Patti offered.

"I'm good," he said. "I should go, though. My mom's on her way home."

Lowell's mom worked as an office cleaner in St. Louis. Her hours were unpredictable, though, and she often had to take extra jobs on the side just so they could get by. His dad, after a long and depressing phase of being unemployed, now worked for the maintenance department in Plattsburgh. I knew that Lowell's parents and Aunt Patti all wanted him to get a job this summer. Money was tight for almost everyone in Plattsburgh, but it was especially tight for Lowell's family. He told me that he wished he could get some kind of job like mine. I also knew that the adults were afraid of him sliding back into Internet world now that I was busy working. So far it hadn't happened.

I rode over to Mr. McCann's extra early the next morning. It had been getting so hot so fast the past few days that I wanted to get most of the work done before the sun reached its maximum roasting power. Mr. McCann paid me by the hour and said it didn't matter which hours I worked as long as I got the jobs done every day. It felt great making my own spending money, and I knew it made things easier for Aunt Patti. First of all, I could pay for the things I did with my friends, or the music I bought, and other things like that. Second of all, there were the Rainy Day expenses that were somewhat beyond our means. Most of the equipment—halter, bridle, saddle, saddle blankets, grooming tools—had been in storage since my parents died, but all his food and medical care added up, and Aunt Patti hated asking my grandma for help. She seemed to think that asking for loans showed her family that she had made a mistake raising me on her own. Grandma, who lived in St. Louis, was always worried about the two of us "out there in the country." She complained that Aunt Patti and I didn't get into town often enough to visit her. As a matter of fact, we hadn't been to St. Louis since early that spring, before I got Rainy Day.

I had been working up the nerve to ask Mr. McCann if he thought he could pay two kids to work around his place. There was definitely enough to do, but the time never seemed right to bring it up. I thought about it as I went through what had become my routine—clearing out stalls, spreading fresh hay, feeding animals, refilling water troughs, piling newspapers to recycle, collecting trash and bagging it for pickup, burying half the kitchen scraps in the compost bin, taking the other half out to the pig, and caring for Hannah.

At nine o'clock, when I was all done, I brought Rainy Day a handful of fresh oats mixed with carrot chunks. He looked up from the grass and nibbled up the snack gratefully. Then he stuck his nose towards my other hand to see if I had any more for him. I scratched him around his white chin hairs and rubbed around his ears.

"You funny boy. Be grateful for what you have. Go play and we'll go home in a little while."

I walked around to the front porch and found Mr. McCann sitting in his chipped and splintered wicker rocker. He was leafing through the newspaper, mumbling reactions to every story. I noticed he was wearing the same clothes as the day before, and I wondered if he was keeping up with his laundry. Mr. McCann picked up a mug whose handle had broken off. The mug said Meramec Caverns across the front and had a wiggly American flag as a background. I knew it was filled with cold black coffee, because sometimes he asked me to go to the kitchen and refill it. In a saucer by his unlaced boot, I saw the stub of a squashed cigarette.

"Morning, April."

"Morning, Mr. McCann."

"What's the buzz from the yard?"

"Mostly the same. I felt the foal kick last night, though. Right before I put Hannah back in her stall. And I forgot to tell you yesterday, but I saw milk on her udder. Drops of milk."

He nodded. "She's waxing, then. Hannah's gone through this before. Three times, matter of fact. She'll know what to do. Still, we better give Marty a call anyway so he can have a look-see."

Marty Smitherman was a horse trainer. Before my parents died he had worked for them at Ozark Pastures. Now he ran a big stable of his own. Marty was one of those people who knew everything about horses. When the tractor-trailer hauling all those horses had crashed back in May, Marty was right there helping in the emergency. For the next several weeks, he had helped me learn what I needed to know to care for Rainy Day, and he had taught me to ride. Marty said it came naturally to me because horses were in my blood, but I knew they would have stayed buried in my blood without Marty's help.

"Get me another slice of that butter cake, will you please, April?" Mr. McCann said. "It's on the kitchen counter."

"Ugh, Mr. McCann. Butter cake?"

"Not one word, Dr. Helmbach," he said, pointing a long finger at me. "Not a word, you hear me?"

I got him the cake and sat down in the wooden chair on the porch. I listened to the rising and falling buzz of the cicadas and the morning chirps of the birds. A big red cardinal landed on top of the mailbox at the end of the front walk.

Mr. McCann ate the cake in three bites. He licked the front and back of the fork, put it down on the plate, and lowered it to the side table. Then he took a noisy sip of cold coffee and wiped his lips with the old hanky he kept in his back pocket. Apart from doing my summer reading, working for Mr. McCann, and taking care of Rainy Day, I had nothing much going on. So I sat for a while with Mr. McCann as he read the newspaper, shaking his head and clucking his tongue over some article he was reading. After a few minutes, he folded the paper into quarters and dropped it on the porch floor.

"You know, April, I'm a lucky man."

"How so?" I asked, watching a black ant hurry along the porch and disappear into a crack in the flooring.

"Sometimes when I'm sitting here I think to myself, some old codger like me that might have sat here a hundred and fifty years ago would be seeing the same things I'm seeing—that dusty brown road, those woods, those birds and bugs flying every which way. Time goes by, but it also doesn't go by."

"But so much happens, Mr. McCann. Time may go by incredibly slowly sometimes, like during health ed, but I never feel like it's not going by at all."

Mr. McCann dug into the front pocket of his work shirt and brought out a crumpled pack of cigarettes. He tapped one end of the pack against the arm of his chair until one cigarette stuck out. Then he pulled it out. I had to bite my tongue to keep from saying anything.

"Oh, now, April, if you keep on goggling at me with those big brown eyes of yours, I'll never be able to do anything that makes me happy again. All right, all right. I won't light up, but there's nothing wrong with having a cigarette in my hand, is there?"

"I guess not," I mumbled.

"You guess not. Well, thank you for your permission."

He put the papery cigarette between his fingers and kept it there. He leaned back in the rocker and whistled a few notes of a song I didn't recognize. His old dog, Buster, a retriever-and-hound mix, came up to the porch and thumped his tail against the porch rail. I patted him on the head, and he lay down across my feet. I thought it might be a good time to ask about Lowell coming to work, too, but before I could get the words out, Mr. McCann started talking.

"It's funny about people, April. When you're young you think everything can be straightened out into neat rows, all black and white, good and bad, right or wrong. Eventually a man grows old, and if he has half a mind, he sees that black and white is an illusion. A wrongheaded illusion at that. If anybody should understand this, it's a person from Missouri, no?" He looked at me.

"What do you mean?" I had no idea why he had brought up this subject at all. "I mean, with what went on in Missouri and even right here in Plattsburgh not even a hundred and fifty years ago."

"Civil War, right? We haven't studied that yet, Mr. McCann. I mean, not in any detail really."

"Not in any detail." Mr. McCann leaned forward in his chair. His eyes were wide and amused. "April, here's a little secret: Life only happens in detail. Nothing in the whole wide world ever happens in general. The minute someone tells you about something or someone *in general*, be suspicious."

Then he leaned back again and switched the unlit cigarette into his other hand. Buster shifted his weight across my feet and sighed. Mr. McCann massaged his left thigh with his free hand and closed his eyes. I could tell he was in pain.

"Lemme tell you something, April. Plattsburgh wasn't a big town in 1861, but it was a town, and just the like rest of Missouri, we were officially pro-Union. We sided with Mr. Lincoln and the North. Slavery was to be abolished, individual freedom was an ideal principle worth fighting for, and a stronger federal government was a good thing. In general." He opened his eyes. "*In general*," he repeated with special emphasis.

"Uh-oh," I said jokingly, remembering what he said about being suspicious of things in general.

"But there were people in Plattsburgh—men, women, and children—who sided with the Confederates of the South. Even if they thought slavery was wrong, they didn't think the federal government ought to butt into the business of the states. You had people in the same town, people going to the same church, having totally opposite points of view."

"That sounds kind of like now," I said. "I actually get confused because some people argue for one side and other people argue for the other side—everyone on both sides is sure they're right."

"Well, it was just the same back then. One old lady, knowing that there were a couple Confederate folks in her church, hung the Union flag across the church doorway so that all those Southern sympathizers who came or went would have to pass under a flag of the opposition."

"But that seems so dumb," I blurted.

"It was dumb, but that's the kind of thing that happened. So this one very annoyed woman refused to walk into church."

"What happened to her?"

"The town officials dragged her off and forced her to take the oath of allegiance to the United States of America. A loyalty oath. Which she did. But afterward—she was a feisty old bird, I guess—she said, 'I said it, but I'll only keep it if I feel like it.'"

I laughed.

"And there's your history for you, April. History in detail, not in general. And I could tell you a few other stories that aren't so plain silly. Or ones where it was someone on the rebel side who did the taunting. But you probably have someplace to go."

I stood up and peered under my shade of the hand toward Rainy Day. He caught my eye and made a quick dash across the paddock, as far away from me as he could get. Clearly, he was in no hurry to leave.

"Not really."

Mr. McCann smiled. "Glad to hear it. So like I said, officially Plattsburgh was a Union town. But there were people everywhere—Burkharts, Bradshaws, Creekmores, Hogans—who sided with the rebels and secretly went around recruiting boys to serve the Southern cause. Old Hogan, he was a college-educated man, and he raised a company and took 'em all south to fight. The battles were terrible, of course, just terrible. One icy night Harry Burkhart and his brother James came trudging back into town. Harry was hurt bad. James was carrying him across his back, carried him across the Bourbeuse River, which was half frozen, if you can believe it. Anyway, James headed straight for old Doc Motherhead's place. Now, Isaac Motherhead was true-blue for the Union, and James knew this as well as anyone when he knocked at the door. Now think about Doc Motherhead: If word got out that he tended to a rebel, it would be considered treason. He had every reason to believe that he could be thrown in jail or shot. Imagine that scene, April."

"I think I know what he did."

"Oh, yeah?"

"He helped the wounded soldier, right?"

"Well, yes, he did. But it wasn't an easy choice."

"It seems like the obvious choice to me."

Mr. McCann raised his eyebrows. "If you've been fighting against slavery, how obvious is it to save a man who'd been fighting to keep people enslaved? My point is that it's obvious from where we sit, maybe, but not so obvious when you're smack in the middle of it, April. Isaac Motherhead risked his own life to save Harry Burkhart's, and he did so knowing that he might be putting another rebel back on the battlefield. I don't care what anybody says, that's not an easy or an obvious thing to do. But it does tell us what kind of a man Isaac Motherhead was, doesn't it?"

"How do you know all this, Mr. McCann?" I asked.

Mr. McCann tipped forward and wiped off the sweat running down his temples. He started coughing and for a minute or two couldn't catch his breath. Eventually he spat into his hanky and crumpled it up in a ball.

"Excuse me," he said. "I was something of a history buff in my day. Had to be. My late wife was a part-time librarian before marrying me, and I spent many an hour hanging around waiting for her. Nothing to do but flip through big old books of firsthand records that nobody ever touched."

"But what difference does any of this make now?" I said. "I'm sorry, Mr. McCann, this was all so long ago."

"April, this may sound like just another lecture, but I know a girl like you can understand. It's the choices we make when we're smack in the middle of things that shows us who we are. The air we breathe is filled with opinions and ideas and points of view—we breathe 'em all. But who we are is what we do, especially what we do when we're around people who are different from us."

Just then I heard a truck coming up the road and looked away from Mr. McCann. The pickup pulled into the gravel drive and came to a stop. Marty got out and waved. He came over to us. Marty had been a jockey when he was young and was very short, but his hands and feet were huge. He put one foot up on the porch and peered up at us through the rails. Buster looked up briefly, thumped his tail once, then put his head down with a sigh.

"Why, I was just going to give you a call," Mr. McCann said. "Looks like it's almost time for old Hannah. At least, according to my able-bodied assistant here. She says Hannah was waxing up yesterday."

"I've been keeping track of the days myself," Marty said. "I wasn't sure you'd be up and about yet, Joe. A foal's a lot of work. Even with April. She's come a long way, that's for sure, but a foaling mare's a whole different ball game. I came to see how I could help."

Mr. McCann started hacking again, and this time, he just couldn't catch his breath. He coughed and coughed, struggling for air. Before he could talk, he waved me and Marty away. I got the picture. He wanted us to clear out.

"I'll show her to you, Marty. Come on." Even though I was really worried about him, I tried to sound relaxed. "I'll see you later, Mr. McCann. Do your therapy."

Marty and I walked out toward the pasture. On my way I grabbed my saddle and saddle pad from off the fence, so I could get Rainy Day ready to go home. Marty went straight to the horses and let out a whoop as he approached Hannah. She and Rainy Day were standing nose to nose in the shade. Their tails swished at flies. I came over and tried to throw the pad across Rainy Day's back, but he practically leaped away from me.

"Hey!" I exploded. "What do you think you're doing? It's time to go home."

I tried again, but he snorted and hopped to the side. I really didn't want Marty to see this, because he always insisted that I be the boss. Disobedience in a horse was not something he allowed.

"Rainy Day, come on," I muttered. "I'm serious. It's

time to go now. All those stories of Mr. McCann's are interesting, but I just can't listen to one more."

Finally I got the saddle pad and saddle onto him. As I adjusted my girth strap, I noticed Marty passing his hands all around Hannah.

"Anytime now," he murmured. "But Lord knows how Joe's going to manage around here."

If I hadn't been too busy trying to stay in control of Rainy Day, who was struggling against me at every step, I would have wondered the same thing myself.

chapter

By the time I got home I was drenched through with sweat and famished for lunch. I unsaddled Rainy Day and gave him water, fresh hay, and a scoop of oats. After the hot trot back home, his eyes brightened once he was in the cool shelter of the barn. I turned on the radio to the hip-hop station we picked up from St. Louis because I sensed Rainy Day liked the steady beat for company.

"See you later, boy."

At this point every day, I had to decide which I was more desperate for—food or a shower. Back in the house, Chase greeted me with happy licks all over my arms. He sniffed my cargoes as if to get a full report of my whereabouts.

Actually, with Aunt Patti at work all day I had everything down to a routine: throw my morning clothes into the washing machine, take out my clean clothes from the drier, and bring them into the bathroom. After a long shower I came out feeling like the day was starting all over again. Then I went into the kitchen to make myself lunch.

I liked the fact that our house was small. Things were

easy to manage. Everything was on one floor—the living room, the dining area, the kitchen, the laundry room, and two small bedrooms. Most of the houses in our part of town were the same size, a little smaller than the garages in the wealthier St. Louis suburbs. Some were in good shape and clean like ours. Others were more run-down and shabby. The one unusual thing about our house was our yard. We had a double lot, and Aunt Patti and I had converted a whole corner into a fenced paddock for Rainy Day. He had his own little prefab barn, fully stocked with everything we needed, and lots of nice green grass. The rest of the yard was landscaped with bushes and flowers that Aunt Patti had been planting and cultivating for the last nine years. Lately she had been saying that the one good thing about the rains and floods, which had practically devastated Plattsburgh in May, was that everything looked better in July than it usually did. "There's enough water in this ground to last us until next spring," she said. "It's nice now that everything that's supposed to be green really is green."

During the floods, a whole section of town—the part with the trailer homes—had been ruined, but by some miracle nobody had died or even been hurt. I was still in semi regular contact with Shawn Clarke, the Iraq veteran I had helped escape from his trailer home. But Shawn told me he was going to be totally preoccupied with studying for college entrance exams all summer and that he'd be more available to get together in the fall.

With the leftovers from dinner the night before, I made myself a flank steak sandwich on a toasted English muffin with mustard, lettuce, and sliced tomato. I put a handful of potato chips on my plate, poured a chilled sports drink into a glass, and sat down at the kitchen table with the August issue of *Horse Lore*.

After lunch, I put my dishes in the dishwasher and started to go back into the living room to watch TV. I plopped down on the couch and reached for the remote on the coffee table when the morning paper caught my eye.

PROTESTERS VOW TO NIX "BUGGY TAX"

Hardly anyone in Plattsburgh protested anything. To tell the truth, I had always thought of Plattsburgh as one of the top ten most boring towns on earth. Nothing ever happened that required protesting, so I couldn't imagine what people would be upset about. The article said there had been a heated discussion at a town council meeting the night before. Something to do with personal property tax and county road maintenance. I didn't have a chance to read more before the phone rang. I was sure it was Aunt

Patti calling to check that I had gotten home okay from Mr. McCann's. She called this time every afternoon.

"Hey. I'm here," I said, somewhat distractedly, staring at a cooking show on which a chef was squirting whipped cream all over some berries.

"Hi, babe," Aunt Patti said. "Everything go okay this morning?"

"Mm-hm."

"That's good. Listen, I need you to come over to the shop."

"Right now?" I said. "I'm exhausted. All I want to do is collapse. It was so hot over there this morning. And I go back around four-thirty. Plus, I told Ruby that I might be able to hang out." Ruby was a girl in my class and a friend, one of my few friends who was nice to Lowell.

"Please, April. I'm not kidding. Now."

"Okay, okay. Like how soon?"

"Like *now* soon. Ride your bike."

I watched the chef sprinkle brown sugar on top of the whipped cream. Then I sighed and turned off the TV. I gave Chase a pat and slipped into flip-flops.

Room for Blooms was about a half block from the center of Plattsburgh, close to the county courthouse and the other official government-type buildings. A lot of Aunt

Patti's business was designing and supplying the flower arrangements for the little restaurants and cafés, and for the people who worked in the offices. She had regular clients, and her specialties were birthdays, weddings, funerals, baby showers, and engagement parties. When big parties or funerals came up, she hired extra people to help her out, but otherwise she was on her own.

I leaned my bike against a parking meter and pushed open the glass door. The bell rang in the back, where Aunt Patti spread everything out on long tables and she kept the huge refrigerator stocked with greens and flowers.

"Hey, hello?" I called.

Aunt Patti's face came through to the front of the shop. She pushed her glasses up on her nose and wiped her wet hands across her dark green apron. I went behind the counter like I always did and sat on the stool at the cash register. Aunt Patti leaned against the counter close by. Behind her was the smaller refrigerator with the glass door. Black plastic buckets held the long-stemmed flowers— roses, daisies, and branches of some kind of bush I didn't know the name of.

"I got a call this morning from Fran," she said. Fran Cheever was Lowell's mother.

"Oh, yeah?"

"Weren't you going to try to see about whether he could work at Mr. McCann's, too?"

"I am. There just hasn't been a good time to bring it up."

"Well, his mom is worried about him again. He was doing so much better after the flood, but she thinks he has too much free time on his hands this summer. It's the same old, same old."

"If you ask me," I said, defending Lowell, "I think Miz Fran should leave him alone. It's vacation."

"I know, but she's worried. Can you please talk to Mr. McCann about it this afternoon?"

"Sure. But did you have me come over here just to ask me about this?"

Aunt Patti smiled. "Well, actually, I need your help. I got a delivery this morning and I can't carry it in all by myself from the alley."

"What kind of delivery?"

"Not too bad." Aunt Patti winked. "Just some moss."

"Moss? Moss is light."

"Not when it's packed into seventy-pound bags, it's not."

I moaned but helped anyway. Aunt Patti thanked me and said she would have dinner ready by the time I got back from Mr. McCann's that evening. I biked home and went into my room. I reached over and opened *Into Thin Air*, one of my pre-eighth grade summer reading books. The people on the expedition were still gathering the supplies needed for their climb up Everest, so the real action hadn't started yet. My eyes were so heavy, I decided to just let them close for two minutes. The next thing I knew, the phone was ringing. It was three-thirty.

This time it was Marty.

"Hey, April. This is it."

"What's it?"

"Come on back to McCann's place. Hannah's foal is on its way. Come straight to her stall."

I leaped out of bed and ran out to the barn. My energy must have startled Rainy Day, because he whinnied and neighed as I entered.

"Sorry, boy," I said, reaching for the saddle pad to toss across his back. "You knew it would be this soon, didn't you?"

He kicked a front hoof into the wooden wall, which I took for an answer.

"So that's why you didn't want to leave this morning. Or yesterday afternoon. You knew Hannah was getting close."

As we rode out of town, I kept thinking about what lay

ahead—a new baby horse on the way. I hoped Mr. McCann would let me be a part of its training. A new horse would mean more work, too. It should be easy to pave the way for Lowell.

After unsaddling Rainy Day and setting him loose in the pasture, I ran into the barn and found Marty standing next to Hannah with a broom in his hand.

"Help me spread fresh hay around, April. She's gonna want a nice clean bed when she lies down."

"How do you know it's time?" I asked him, taking the pitchfork and stabbing a clump from the bundle of dry hay stuffed inside the iron rack.

"I never left this morning. Hung around doing this and that. When I heard she was waxing up I knew it would be any time, and old Joe's in no kind of shape to monitor the birth, much as he won't admit it. I told him I'd stay on and come right over to tell him when it was over."

"What's waxing up?" I asked.

"What you saw yourself. It's when the first drops of milk come and start to crystallize. That usually means the foal's on its way inside twenty-four hours."

Hannah seemed nervous and fidgety. She kept turning her head around toward her back end and swishing her long black tail like a whip, retangling the long hair I had brushed out that very morning.

"And look at this," Marty said. "Keep your distance but come stand behind her. See how she's hollowing out along the withers? Right down on either side of her spine you can see her changing shape. That's because the birth canal is opening up. Sometimes I wrap the tail up in a bandage to keep it out of the way but I'm not gonna do that today. All depends on the mare. Hannah's been through this and we're just here to see that she does her thing, nice and normal."

Even though I had learned so much about horses since May, I was a little freaked out. I had never seen a human or animal birth, and never heard any stories about my own birth—how long it took, what it was like, how nervous or excited my parents were, the things that went wrong on the way to the hospital. All my friends seemed to know those kinds of stories. When both your parents die, you never get that information. All I knew was what my relatives had told me way after the fact, but they didn't know anything firsthand. There I was about to see a huge animal having a baby and I had no idea what to expect. Would it be scary? Bloody? How long would it take? What if something went wrong?

Hannah seemed completely unaware of us. I put down the pitchfork and went to stand next to Marty. He stood with his hands on his hips and never took his eyes off Hannah.

Suddenly Hannah lay down on the hay and stretched out on her right side. A gush of clear watery liquid poured out around her bottom and just a second or two later I saw her tail lift up. Something white poked out from between her hind legs.

"Here we go," Marty said. "Front legs come first, with the nose lying down on top."

"What's that white stuff?" I asked.

"Amniotic sac. Water's broken but the foal's still inside it."

I vaguely remembered hearing about the amniotic sac in biology. Somehow I didn't picture it so thick and white. A little section of the sac had torn away from the foal's nose.

Seconds later Hannah stiffened out her rear legs like a soldier. Unbent at every joint, they stretched out perpendicular to her body.

"That's how you know she's pushing," Marty said.

Out came the shoulders and midsection of the foal. Hannah's legs stayed stiff and stretched out for another minute or two as she pushed out the rest of the foal. Marty went over to her. Bending down near the foal's head, he reached over and made the tiny opening in the sac a little bigger so that its whole face was in the open air. Now I could see the nose more clearly. It was brown like Hannah's, with legs shading to a darker brown toward the hooves. Marty stepped back to me. More of the sac tore away and I could see the foal's ribs. It was so skinny. Another minute went by and then its hips and back legs appeared, first one and then the other. At the same time, Hannah relaxed her rear legs, rolled onto her stomach, and turned to face her foal. I couldn't believe how fast it had happened. Three or four minutes and here was a new baby horse! The head was out in the open but the rest of its body was still inside the sac. I stood paralyzed, like a tree rooted to the barn floor.

"It's something, isn't it?" Marty murmured.

"I didn't expect it to be so fast," I said.

"It's got to be fast. The umbilical cord breaks when it's still inside. Once it breaks, the foal's got no source of oxygen. It's got to get out in order to breathe."

"Is it a he or a she?" I asked.

"Well, let's see."

Marty leaned back down and pulled and tugged the sac away from the foal. When he got it in a big heavy lump, he used the pitchfork to toss it in a bucket. He did this so quickly, I didn't even notice him checking the foal.

"A boy," he said. "A colt-to-be. Congratulations, Hannah." He gave her a pat.

The foal had not stopped moving. He was flicking his ears as his front legs folded back. His back legs were bent in sharp angles.

"His legs seem impossibly long."

"Crazy long," Marty said.

"What if you hadn't been here to move the sac out of the way?"

"Mares'll do it with their teeth. In fact, most mares give birth in the middle of the night and that's exactly what they do. In some cases they'll go ahead and eat the sac. I asked a vet about it a long time ago, and he said that's what they do in the wild. It keeps the scent of the foal and the birth from predators."

"Now what?" I asked, sliding down to the floor of the barn. I was still trying to believe what I had just seen: a whole new horse joining the world.

"Now we wait," Marty said. "A couple of things have to happen. This kid's got to get control of his legs to stand up and nurse, and Hannah's got to pass the afterbirth. The placenta."

Hannah shifted her weight and nosed toward the foal

as he wriggled toward her. Marty and I sat and watched and didn't say much. The rest of the animals in the barn never quieted down. The pig snorted, the chickens clucked, and the goats bleated. Meanwhile, the foal seemed surprised to be able to move. His eyes were big and bright, and every so often he stopped moving and sat still, listening and looking, as if it was just too hard to keep going when there was so much to hear and see. After about twenty minutes, he got himself up with his legs all splayed out every which way. Hannah stood also and helped support him with her muzzle.

"Here we go," Marty said, groaning as he also rose to his feet.

The foal was so small, he could have walked under Hannah's belly. He stuck his head forward under her and began to nurse.

"Just the way it's supposed to go," Marty said, smiling. "And believe me, April, it's a lot nicer when it turns out this way. I've been around stillbirths and other bad turnouts and those are no fun. You're lucky," he said, before turning to look at me for the first time since the birth. "April? You okay?"

I think I must have been in some kind of trance. The whole world was filled with animals, and all of them had

had to be born, which meant that being born was an everyday thing. Still, I knew what I had just seen was not an everyday thing. I was sure I would never forget it.

Somehow I went about my chores as usual that afternoon. Marty left the barn and went to report to Mr. McCann that everything had gone well. I took as many breaks as I could to go pat Hannah and the foal, who was the cutest thing I had ever seen. His head only came up to my waist, and his body moved like a little marionette. Hannah eventually passed the placenta, which Marty tossed in with the sac to throw away. Before leaving the farm, I went into the house and gave Mr. McCann a hug.

"You're a grandfather," I said.

"Watch it, missy," he said. "I may be a monkey's uncle, but I'll never be a horse's papa."

I laughed. "See you tomorrow. What a day."

"Thanks for everything, Doc Helmbach," he said. "I'm glad you were here."

"Me, too, Mr. McCann."

chapter

4

"Lucky you, April. I'm jealous," Aunt Patti said when I got home and had put Rainy Day in for the night. Aunt Patti was at the sink, scrubbing dirt off potatoes. "I've always wanted to see a live birth," she said. "The only animal I've ever seen born are gerbils, and that was when I was little, too young to appreciate it. I thought it was disgusting."

"Well, all that blood and placenta was kind of intense, but the little foal was so amazing. He was all legs and eyes. And his tail was so short—like a squirrell's tail."

By the time we were done eating and cleaning up dinner I was exhausted and went straight to bed. Before falling asleep, I thought about the rest of the summer. I wondered how the foal would change my routine. I hadn't had a chance to ask Mr. McCann about hiring Lowell, but it definitely seemed more likely he would need extra help.

As Rainy Day and I approached Mr. McCann's place the next morning, I noticed two extra cars in the gravel driveway. One was Marty's truck, which didn't surprise me, but the other one was a silver sedan that I didn't recognize. It wasn't a Plattsburgh kind of car.

"You be nice to Hannah today, Rainy Day," I said, unsaddling him and switching his bridle for a halter. "Keep your distance until you're sure she wants your company."

Rainy Day nodded his head up and down. It was the kind of gesture he made all the time, but every so often it seemed like an actual response to what I had said. I rubbed his neck and gave him a kiss on his scarred cheek. He blew air out his nostrils and trotted off to graze.

"April!"

It was Marty calling, and I turned toward the barn.

"No, over here. I'm on the porch. Come here."

Something about the expression on Marty's face scared me. I knew I ought to be moving faster, but I walked over as slowly as I could.

"Is the foal okay?"

"Foal's fine, April. It's something else."

Before he could go on, a man in a white dress shirt and rumpled business suit came out of the front door. He was talking on Mr. McCann's phone. He saw me and half waved, then walked to the far end of the porch, still talking in a low voice.

"Who's that?" I asked.

"That's Nelson McCann, Mr. McCann's son. He just came out from St. Louis a couple minutes ago."

"St. Louis? But—"

"April, Mr. McCann passed in his sleep last night," Marty said. He put his hand on my shoulder.

At first I didn't understand what Marty meant by "passed." Passed where? Passed what? I was blanking out.

"You mean he died?" I asked, still unsure of what was happening.

"The doctor said he had a blood clot that got stuck in his heart. He died very quickly. No pain, no suffering."

"But when? How? He seemed fine last night. Did he get to see Hannah and her foal?" I couldn't believe what I was asking. It seemed impossible to think Mr. McCann was gone.

"Well, I don't think he saw them, no," Marty said. "But he did know how everything turned out. The doctor said one thing just led to another, that these things can happen after hip operations. There was nothing anyone could have done."

I nodded, but I kept my thoughts to myself. One thing may have led to another, but all I could think about was Mr. McCann dragging on those cigarettes. If he had done what he was supposed to do, would one thing have led to another? No doubt I should have burst into tears, but I'm ashamed to admit that the first thing I felt was mad—mad at Mr. McCann. It was wrong of him not to take better care of himself. I could tell Marty was watching me closely, but he kept quiet, too.

Nelson McCann said good-bye to whoever he was talking to. He walked over and Marty told him who I was.

"Glad to meet you," he said, extending his hand.

"Hi," I said. Shaking Mr. McCann's son's hand made me feel less angry and more sad. The fact was, his dad had died, and suddenly it didn't seem to matter how.

"I'm really sorry about Mr. McCann," I said. Looking at Nelson, I was surprised at how well dressed and urban he seemed compared to his farmer dad.

"Do you mind if we sit down for a minute?" he said.

Marty leaned back against the porch rail and folded his arms across his chest. I sat in the wooden chair I always sat in, and Nelson plopped down in Mr. McCann's rocker. He leaned back and looked out toward the road just like Mr. McCann used to do. In spite of his totally different clothes and age, I could see the resemblance between father and son.

Nobody said anything for a while. I guessed Nelson to be about the same age as Aunt Patti, which would make him a little more than thirty. He had hardly any beard, but did have thick sandy hair. He had gray eyes that looked friendly but tired, and his face was pale. Suddenly he leaned forward.

"You know, Pop left me a message about Hannah," he said. "I heard it on my way out around four this morning. He must have called after eleven because I turn off the ringer when I go to bed."

"Doctor said it happened after midnight, closer to two or three," Marty said.

Nelson nodded. "I had just gotten into law school when the folks got Hannah," he said. "She was six years old, and I had just graduated from college and said good-bye to Plattsburgh. I think Pop thought he could lure me back with a nice sweet filly. At least, that was what my brothers and sisters said."

Nelson stopped talking for a second and covered his face with his hands. Seeing him deal with his pain triggered the old familiar sadness I had over my own parents and I also started to well up. Fighting back a full meltdown, I made myself think of the one thing that always made me feel better—riding Rainy Day down a country road. After a minute Nelson lowered his hands and looked up at me.

"I really appreciate everything you've done around here since May. I know Pop was really grateful you could help him out. He can be a little difficult to deal with at times."

"A little," I agreed. "But you get used to it."

Marty slapped himself on the thighs and cleared his throat. "April, it's gonna be a little hectic around here for a few days, but the animals still need what they need. The foal for one'll need as much contact with humans as we can give him. Why don't you call your aunt Patti and let her know what's happened, then get going on what you need to get done."

I stood and started to walk away. If there was something appropriate to do or say at that point, I had no idea what it was. I felt like a zombie—all I was able to do was follow directions.

"Oh, and one other thing," Marty said. "Feel free to get your hands on that foal, assuming Hannah'll let you. Starting right now, he needs to get used to being touched and handled. Only watch out for his hind legs. It'll be his instinct to practice a little self-defense."

"As in kicking?" I asked, imaging a sharp jab to the thigh.

"That's right. But hang on. You should call your aunt Patti first."

It was Aunt Patti who burst into tears when I told her

the news. From the porch where I was sitting talking on the phone, I could see Rainy Day grazing peacefully. I had to squint because the morning sun was shining in my eyes. Hannah and her foal were standing about ten yards away from Rainy Day. Hannah was nibbling grass, and the foal was trying to copy her. But his legs were so long—or maybe his neck was so short—he couldn't reach the grass. Eventually, as I sat there, I watched him give up. He tucked his head under Hannah and began to nurse.

"Oh, April, how horrible. Are you okay?"

"I'm okay. At least I think I am. I've got stuff to do. There's the foal, of course. And Hannah." I debated whether or not to tell Aunt Patti that I suspected Rainy Day had tried to get me to stretch out my visit yesterday morning, but decided to let it go.

"One of Mr. McCann's sons is here," I said. "I think his name is Nelson."

The phone went quiet.

"Aunt Patti?"

"Hmmm?"

"Okay, just checking you're there. I gotta go."

Later that morning I was shoveling out Hannah's stall when Nelson McCann came out to the barn and leaned against the rail. He had changed his clothes, and in jeans and a T-shirt he looked a lot younger.

"Hey," he said, knocking on the splintered wood of the rail.

"Hi."

"What a surreal day," he said. "I keep thinking, there's no practicing or warm-up for something like this. Your parents only die once, and that's the real thing."

"I know," I said.

"Listen, April, Marty told me about your folks. I know it's been a while, but, well, I'm sorry."

"It's okay," I said, shifting the wheelbarrow so I could reach into a corner with the shovel.

"Well, it's not okay, but you're okay. And that's the important thing, right?"

"I guess so," I said, not adding that actually I was okay ninety-nine percent of the time, and that Rainy Day helped get me through the one percent. Nelson didn't really need to know that.

For a couple of seconds Nelson beat a little rhythm on the stall door with both hands. I thought he was about to say good-bye and leave, but he kept standing there.

"You know," he said, "I went to school with your aunt Patti. Patti Helmbach, right?"

"Right," I confirmed.

"She was the only kid in our class who beat me every time on every test. And in fifth grade during the chess craze, she beat me at that, too. Every game but one. That's the one I like to remember."

I stopped working and looked up. Nelson winked. "I haven't seen her since...I don't know when," he said. He fell silent, and again I thought he was about to leave. He actually turned to go, but then wheeled around.

"You know, I always had a mad crush on Patti Helmbach. Inappropriate line of questioning—is she still cute?"

Rattled, I wasn't sure how to respond. Nelson smiled.

"Sorry. I guess that's a weird thing to say on a day like today. But I have to admit, I can't tell what's weird and not weird right now. The world feels upside down with Pop gone."

"I guess so," I said, realizing that this was a good opportunity to break the tension we both felt. "I mean, I guess she's still cute."

Nelson and I both laughed.

"Anyway," he said. "I have to stay by the house because my cell has no coverage out here and the whole world is calling. I'll try to get back out to the barn a little later."

I returned to my chores. I cleaned and swept stalls,

scattered fresh feed around the poultry yard, and kept an eye on the foal. Sometimes he was standing. Other times he seemed to be sound asleep at Hannah's feet. After an hour Nelson returned. He said he wanted to see what had to be done, but I think he needed a break from everything going on inside the house.

"What do you do in St. Louis?" I asked.

Nelson explained that he was a lawyer with the public defender's office.

"Huh," I said, puzzled. "So what do you actually do?"

"Everyone accused of a crime is entitled to be represented by an attorney," he said. "People who can't afford to hire their own lawyer get one assigned to them from my office. So that's what I do. I defend people in court."

"That's cool," I said.

"I like the work," Nelson said, "but it's a little draining after half a dozen years. People do such stupid things, and even if they haven't done the stupid thing they're accused of doing, chances are they've done some other stupid thing nobody knows about. And all because everything that can go wrong in their lives has gone wrong and they're just trying to survive day to day."

"Sounds depressing."

"It can be. Some days I feel like a slimeball, other days

like a knight in shining armor." He looked at me and smiled.

Old Moses, Mr. McCann's hog, strolled in from the hot sun. He went over to his trough to see what I had put inside. Nelson picked up a stick and scratched old Moses on the back.

"Didn't you want to be a farmer like your dad?" I asked.

"In a word, April, no. When I left Plattsburgh to go to college, I knew I'd never come back. Look at me. Do I look like the kind of person cut out for backbreaking labor from dawn to dusk?" I could tell Nelson was trying to be jokingly self-deprecating, but he also sounded bitter. It reminded me of how Lowell had sounded earlier that year when his dad had been giving him a hard time.

"Oh, I don't know," I said. "I think anyone can be cut out for backbreaking labor if they like backbreaking labor."

"Oh-ho," Nelson said. "So you're one of those clever kids we adults hear so much about, aren't you?"

"There's a lot of us floating around," I said, joking right back.

"Well, then I'll have to think about it, I guess," he said, passing me the stick so I could continue scratching old Moses. "It's nice out here, but I need to go confirm more of the funeral arrangements. Family is coming to town from every point on the compass."

An hour later Aunt Patti showed up with a big cooler full of sandwiches, cookies, and drinks. I heard her car pull up and was actually relieved to see that she went straight into the house. I didn't really want to go back in by myself. Instead I wandered out to the paddock where Rainy Day was grazing alone. He perked up when he saw me, approached at a trot, and buried his nose under my shoulder.

"Hey, buddy," I said. "You were trying to get me to spend as much time as possible here yesterday, weren't you? Did you know that would be Mr. McCann's last night? Or did you sense Hannah was ready to foal?"

He swished his tail and threw his head up. I patted him all around his face and scratched behind his ears. "And here I thought I was in tune with you...." I murmured. "I gotta do a better job of paying attention."

I gave Rainy Day one last pat and wandered over to the house. I found Aunt Patti and Nelson sitting side-by-side, eating tuna sandwiches.

They had already made plans for Aunt Patti to do the flowers for the funeral, which would be in two days, and now they were reminiscing. I helped myself to a sandwich and a soda and listened. Aunt Patti was explaining how her life had unfolded—how she was raising me and living in Plattsburgh. As I listened, I wondered if Nelson still thought she was cute.

"So when Mary Beth and Harry died, it just seemed like the right thing to do," Aunt Patti said. "I put off graduate school and moved out here to Plattsburgh, where they'd been running Ozark Pastures."

"I remember that place," Nelson said. "It was nice."

"The nicest around," Aunt Patti said. "I sold it, though, and bought the little house we're in now. I put the rest of that money in bonds for April here."

"Wait," Nelson said. "You mean you just went straight from college to having a four-year-old?"

"That's what I did." She reached over and squeezed my leg. "And I've never had a day of regret in my life."

"I imagine you haven't," Nelson said, which made me feel slightly embarrassed. There was something about the look on his face and his tone of voice that made me feel like he was paying both of us a compliment.

Aunt Patti took the paper napkins and garbage into the house to throw away. When she came back she had her hands on her hips.

"The house is a disaster area," she said. "But I guess

you know that already. I think I'll stay the afternoon and get things pulled together before the rest of your family shows up."

"I told you Mr. McCann pretty much let everything go," I said. "It's been a mess for a while, ever since the flood in May. But at least he ate lots of gooey butter cake at the end."

Nelson and Aunt Patti laughed, but my eyes teared up thinking about those last conversations I had had with Mr. McCann. Had I been too hard on him about smoking and doing his exercises? Should I have been harder all along? And I still had questions about his Civil War stories about taking sides, and about figuring out whether it was possible to have opposite opinions at the same time. Only one thing was certain: Life and death would always be on different sides. But maybe that was one of those generalities he had tried to warn me against. Aunt Patti's voice brought me back to the moment.

"So how come *you're* not married, Nelson?" Aunt Patti said, not mincing words.

"I don't know," Nelson said. "One thing at a time, I guess. I left the country because I didn't feel I belonged here, but it's hard to find someone who can understand what it means to grow up in a place like Plattsburgh. I focused completely on work. Now even that is worrying me. I guess I'm at loose ends about what's going on in my life professionally." He chuckled. "I don't know. I'm too young for a midlife crisis and too old to be so confused."

"And now your father died," Aunt Patti said, which seemed slightly *too* direct to me, but not, evidently, to Nelson. He shrugged and smiled sadly.

"My father just died," he repeated, as if he had to say the words himself to believe them. "You know, I have no idea what's going to happen now. I've called in to work and said I'd be gone the rest of the week."

Nobody said anything for a few minutes. Aunt Patti swept the front steps, which were caked with dried mud.

"How about you come over for dinner tonight?" she suggested.

Nelson looked up at her and said, "You're on."

chapter

It was getting late, and I closed *You and Your Horse* over my finger to mark my place. Slow music and the soft tones of Aunt Patti's and Nelson's lowered voices drifted from the living room to where I lay on my bed reading. I couldn't make out what they were saying, only that they hadn't stopped talking since dinner was over.

Lowell had come for dinner, too. He took to Nelson right away. Maybe it was because Nelson was kind and funny, but also because they seemed to have a few things in common. The last few years, Lowell had been having a hard time in school because he didn't fit into any of the little tiny boxes that middle school tries to push you into. He wasn't a jock and he wasn't a geek. He always felt that his dad would have been more proud of him if he had been a star football player. Starting in sixth grade, Lowell got all doughy and soft, which made things even harder for him. Since the flood in May, he had been working hard to get into shape. Maybe that had something to do with why he was less cynical than he had been for the past few years. I sensed that it was good for Lowell to meet people who weren't your typical Plattsburgh townies.

The book in my hand was a heavy hardback. I had checked it out of the library weeks and weeks ago, renewing it over the phone when it came due. The author was someone called N. J. Farragut. I couldn't tell whether that was a man or a woman, but I had my suspicions. Kind of like what I had once read about J. K. Rowling, who supposedly used initials so nobody would know whether she was female or male. Actually, I hoped N. J. Farragut was a woman. I had been imagining her as my very own trainer speaking to me from the pages of a book written back in 1957. Along with Marty's help, I had been depending on N. J. Farragut for the details of taking care of Rainy Day. Now I would need it for the foal, too.

I glanced over at *Into Thin Air* and felt guilty. I had abandoned the climbers before they even started up the mountain. When would I get around to my summer reading? Not tonight, I thought, sticking a random three of clubs into page 265 of *You and Your Horse* and putting it on the nightstand.

Early the next morning, I rode over to Mr. McCann's like it was any other day. It was too weird not to call the place "Mr. McCann's." I just wasn't ready to face the fact that he wasn't going to be there waiting to make mean cracks. It was like Marty said, even though the animals might sense something was different, they still needed everything they always did—food to eat, water to drink, clean places to lie down. I still had to collect the eggs, shovel away muck, and spread clean hay. The list of chores went on and on.

Hannah and her foal stood in the cool darkness of their stall. The foal was nursing, and Hannah was looking absently out the window while chewing on dry hay. The barn swallows were already up and swooping around under the eaves where they had built their nests, gathering bits of hay and whatever else they did that made them seem so busy.

"Morning, Hannah. Morning, baby," I said. At the sound of my voice, the foal jumped away from Hannah and looked at me. He backed away on his spindly legs and stood on the far side of his dam. Seeing alarm in his eyes, I tried to speak soothingly.

"Hey, remember me? I was here when you were born."

"Horses aren't born, April, they're foaled."

I jumped at the sound of Marty's voice. I hadn't even heard him come in.

"Or you could even say they're dropped. Might as well

get the words right."

"Got it," I said. "Foals are foaled. You scared me, Marty."

"Sorry. Been here since four. First couple of days are super important. Don't want anything to go wrong out here just because everything's topsy-turvy in there." He jerked his head toward the house. "Besides, I couldn't sleep. Kept thinking there was something I coulda done for old Joe when I first got here yesterday morning. Some resuscitation or something."

Marty was in the stall now. He had the foal's head tucked under his arm. With his free hand, he was patting Hannah, who always looked a little suspicious when anyone came near her foal. I watched his movements closely so I could do what he was doing when he left.

"Turns out there wasn't anything anybody coulda done," Marty went on, rubbing the foal under his chin. "I ran into the doctor at the hospital—they called me right away 'cause old Joe kept my number on his phone—and he told me so himself. Said Joe had what's called a saddle embolus, if you can believe it. Blood clot started in his leg, went up to the heart, and got stuck heading out of the heart toward his lungs. Says that place between heart and artery is called a saddle. He might have felt a second of pain, but it was over quickly. Nothing anyone coulda done. After I heard that I went home and fell asleep. For a coupla hours anyway."

"Well, I'm here to do my job," I said. "You can go home, if you want."

"Maybe I will. I got a pile a mile high on my desk and fifteen other animals to think about. Wait, though, I need to grab something from the truck."

Marty came back with a sheepskin halter. It was the tiniest halter I had ever seen.

"For the foal?" I asked.

"We'll try it at the end of the day. Only for a minute or two, and just to get him used to the idea. But you may as well let him sniff at it this morning."

I took the soft little halter and stuffed it into my back pocket.

"One other thing before I go, April."

Marty pulled a section of rope off a hook on the wall and stepped around into the stall. He kept the rope in a loop and let the foal smell it. Then he gently brushed it along his back, head to tail. Just once. He did the same to Hannah, who paid no attention. Then he brushed the foal's nose with two fingers, murmured in his ear, and came back out of the stall.

"Do that a couple times over the morning."

"What was 'that'? What did you say to him?"

Marty chuckled, and it was the first time I had seen him amused in days.

"Sorry. You've taken to all this so natural, I forget you weren't born and raised in a barn. You want a foal to feel comfortable with all the things he's going to need to accept eventually. He's not a blank slate, exactly. Horses have personalities like people. But he can and will learn what's in store for him if we show him what's what from the start. Getting him used to the smell and feel of a rope is a good thing to do at this point. I just whispered that he should think of the rope as his friend, or something like that. Can't quite remember exactly how I put it."

"Like Black Beauty and the trains," I said, remembering the story I had read for the first time when I got Rainy Day.

Marty looked doubtful. I know he didn't approve of book knowledge apart from hands-on experience.

"I mean, Black Beauty talks about how his first owner was so smart because he made Black Beauty stand in a part of a meadow pasture not far from the train tracks. He was put in that pasture with a bunch of cows and sheep, who didn't respond at all when the trains shrieked by. At first Black Beauty was alarmed, but when he saw that the trains never left the track, and noticed that the other animals never seemed to mind the loud noises, he just grew used to it, too, and trains never bothered him again."

Marty chuckled. "I guess it's close to the same thing. Any of us animals can get used to just about anything if we have no choice about it. So just go ahead and do what I did."

Marty left and I got to work, but every few minutes I couldn't resist stopping by Hannah's stall to pet the foal. One time I must have moved too quickly behind him on my way out. I had just turned my back when I felt a sharp kick on the back of my thighs. It wasn't that hard, but I knew I'd probably have a bruise.

"Hey!"

The foal stood his ground and stared at me. Hannah didn't budge. I knew there was probably something I should have done to teach him never to do that again, and I was certain that Marty and N. J. Farragut knew what that something was, but I didn't. Black Beauty had never kicked anyone in his life. "Never bite or kick, even in play," was his mother's advice. But I didn't feel like teaching anyone anything just then. Rubbing the back of my legs, I just walked out of the stall.

chapter

Around ten o'clock, Nelson came out and met me by the compost heap. I was burying all the slop that old Moses hadn't eaten in the last few days.

"Morning," he said.

"Hey," I replied, ignoring the musky, ashy odor that rose from the damp and steaming pile of decomposing leaves, plants, and food.

Nelson jerked his thumb toward the barn. "You know, that little guy in there needs a name."

I stabbed the shovel into the dark pile of compost and turned to face Nelson. "You mean the foal?"

"I do indeed. I don't feel up to it myself."

"Wow. Cool." I was totally psyched to name Hannah's foal. "Thanks, Nelson. Can I take a little time?"

"Sure you can. I just wanted to make the offer. Think you can do it in a day or two?"

"I'll try."

We stood and looked out at the horses in the fenced pasture. Hannah and the foal stood together in a patch of long grass. Rainy Day was walking toward them slowly. He nodded to me on his way, as if to say how happy he was this morning. He broke into a trot and came right up to Hannah. She nickered and swished her tail.

"What are you doing in there?" I asked.

"Basically digging through junk," Nelson said. "Pop's so-called office is beyond belief, and I'm trying to write an obituary for the newspaper, but there's more information than I can deal with. He did more than I ever knew. Plus, the attic is filled with clippings, papers, and stuff. None of this takes into account how everything seems to be broken or falling apart—the kitchen sink is dripping, the windows in the bedrooms won't open, the attic ceiling is cracking from wall to wall, and the fireplaces are all filled with old half-charred logs. My mom would have had a fit if she saw her house this way."

This was the opening I'd been waiting for.

"Nelson, you know my friend Lowell? From last night?"

Nelson nodded and I continued enthusiastically.

"Well, he could really use a summer job, and I thought maybe he could—"

"Sign him up," Nelson interrupted. "Tell him I can pay him by the hour and he can work as many hours as he can tolerate. Starting this afternoon. There are going to be droves of people gathering in the next day or so, and I'd hate to see them thinking that Pop let things go this badly. After the funeral the work won't feel so desperate, I'm sure, but we'll still need help."

I jumped off the fence rail. I couldn't wait to call Lowell. I wasn't sure how thrilled he would be with the actual job, but I knew he would appreciate the money part.

"Thanks a ton, Nelson. This is great. You have no idea."

Before Nelson turned to go, he told me to come inside when Lowell got there so he could show us the attic. "Come straight upstairs. You're not going to believe it."

I called Lowell and told him about Nelson's offer.

"I'm not so good at all that handyman stuff," he said.

"It's fine," I assured him. "I'm sure it's nothing you couldn't pick up. Can your mom give you a ride over soon, like now?"

"Now?"

Lowell was one of those people who like to mull things over forever before making a commitment, but sometimes he needed a direct and immediate command. Luckily, his mom was right there talking to him in the background.

"See you," I said, and hung up.

Nelson was right. The attic was a mess. We were all standing in the dusty, hot, low-ceilinged room, where the stacks of yellowing newspapers were knee-high all around us. Lowell sneezed.

"And this isn't all," Nelson said. "Check this out."

He pointed to a whole separate pile of local papers dedicated to Plattsburgh's centennial celebration back in the 1950s.

"Read it," he commanded.

To our amazement, it turned out that Mr. McCann had been on the town council. He had been head of the committee that organized the celebration and was quoted all through the paper. No wonder he knew so much about history. Not only that but we found another whole stack of papers with articles Mr. McCann had written himself, stories about Plattsburgh history and current farming practices. He had written editorials, too. One argued for holding on to the town's identity even as neighboring towns began to get swallowed up by the western expansion of St. Louis. One year he had even run for mayor but lost.

"Looks like your dad was a play-a, Nelson," Lowell said, after reading aloud a couple paragraphs from one of these articles. "A play-a."

"I wonder why he never told us kids about all this," Nelson said, sitting on a bent stool with an open newspaper across his lap. I liked the way he ignored Lowell's dumb hip-hop impression. Nelson kept talking as he leafed through the papers and files. "He was really into all this civic pride stuff. And I thought I was the first person in this house to go into public service."

Why Mr. McCann kept his accomplishments a secret didn't make any sense but then a thought came to me.

"Maybe we should name the foal Joseph," I said quietly. "After your dad. Or Joe, or Joey. Something like that. Mr. McCann loved Hannah so much, and he never even got to meet the foal. And none of us are ever going to be able to think about this week without remembering Mr. McCann anyway."

Nelson looked up at me. "Well, Pop's middle name was Palmer, named from his mother's side of the family. Joey makes me think of baby kangaroos. How do you feel about JP as a name?"

"Hannah and JP," I said, trying out the sound. "JP 'Whoa, JP.' Yeah, I think it works."

"So there we go. One thing accomplished anyway," Nelson said. "Now let's divide and conquer. April, you stay up here." He got up and shoved three huge cardboard boxes into the center of the attic. "Put anything that he either wrote or is about him in this one. Put all other papers in this one. And put everything you find that's trash—broken stuff, old pens, tools with missing parts—in this one."

"But Nelson, I need to get back to the barn," I said, not wanting to get sucked into sorting when I could be with the foal. "I'm meeting Marty there in an hour."

"You'll be done in an hour," he said. "And if you're not, just leave it and come back. Lowell, you come downstairs. You're on vacuum detail. Me, I'll see about getting these windows to function. I don't think they've been opened in years."

Lowell saluted Nelson and whirled on his heel to follow him downstairs. I grabbed him by the elbow.

"Hey, don't be a jerk," I said.

"Sorry," Lowell said. "I'll try, but it's not easy."

Whenever Lowell acted like a wise guy, it always turned out he had mixed feelings about something. Maybe he felt I had ganged up on him to make him work, even though he did need to earn his own money and was glad to do so. Maybe a part of him got sick of the fact that I wasn't hung up on being cool. Or maybe he didn't know how to act around Nelson in those first days after Mr. McCann died.

The next few days passed in a blur. Between taking care of the animals, helping Nelson fix up the house, and running around for Aunt Patti as she prepared the flowers for the funeral, I hardly had time to think. I met all kinds of McCann relatives, some who stayed in the house with Nelson, some who found room with old friends, and others who checked into the Restful Lodge on I-54. Casseroles and cakes had collected in the kitchen, covering every inch of the counter. Two of these I brought home for me and Aunt Patti. The others, I admit, I ended up feeding to old Moses. During quiet moments, I hung out in the stall with Hannah and her foal, watching them together. Even when Hannah seemed to be eating or paying attention to Rainy Day, who liked to hang out right near the window, I could tell she knew exactly what the foal was doing. Seeing the two of them so connected to each other, I couldn't help but feel that tiny gnawing pain that reminded me that I had had such a short time with my own mother. Luckily, the feeling passed in the rush of daily life. In a way it was comforting to see how life went on for the animals no matter what, at least as long as we all kept taking care of them.

Mr. McCann's funeral was brief and simple, and I felt sure he would have been pleased with the ceremony. The pastor called him a "solid citizen in the best sense," which seemed true to me. Afterwards Aunt Patti, Lowell, and I rode together to the cemetery and stood by when they lowered the casket into the ground. Aunt Patti gripped my hand so tightly I thought she would cut off my circulation. I'm pretty sure she was thinking about my parents' funeral and worrying about me. I squeezed her hand back, trying to tell her I was fine. I actually did feel fine.

It didn't hit me what a vacuum there was until the first day I went over to the McCann farm after the funeral. Without Mr. McCann, the place felt empty. Nobody to crack bad jokes or tease me about being a doctor. Nobody there telling stories about the old days just because he felt like it.

The hot sunny days followed one right after another, and Lowell and I fell into a routine. I still rode Rainy Day over to McCann's really early in the morning, while he got a ride from his mom or Aunt Patti closer to nine o'clock. We brought our own lunches and ate either in the house or on the front porch. Sometimes Nelson was there; other times he was in town settling the details of the estate. He always left Lowell a long to-do list and laid out any tools he thought Lowell might need. Buster hung out with us, too. I think he needed the company.

I had been doing my best to get JP into a routine. Sometimes he leaned into me with his shoulder, pushing me away from Hannah. Other times I could tell he liked having me around because he enjoyed the massages and scratches. Still, he was not thrilled about the fuzzy halter. Mostly he wanted to bite it. And he definitely did not want it pulled over his head. What did my teachers say about us seventh graders? That we were "a work in progress." JP was definitely a work in progress.

One Sunday morning toward the end of July, I was squatting down by Hannah's left front leg, gently scrubbing out underneath her hoof. The rising and falling buzz of insects was all I could hear, except for an occasional curse from Lowell, who was trying to mend a section of rotting and broken fence Marty had pointed out to Nelson. That part of the fence lay right along the road in front of the house. Nobody had noticed it was down because a bunch of weeds was blocking the view.

Hannah had her eye on JP, who must have been feeling brave and independent that morning. He was standing with Rainy Day in the shade, not too far from Lowell but several yards away from Hannah. He and Rainy Day watched Lowell struggle with the lumber and wire as if they couldn't understand why a person would be trying to do something that plainly made him so furious. The strong fencing wire lay in a stiff coil beside him.

For no apparent reason, JP reared back onto his long and bony hind legs and started running in circles, stretching his little tail back in the air. He came over to Hannah, nudged her with his muzzle, then ran back to Rainy Day. Bumblebees were dipping in and out of the wildflowers along the fence, and white butterflies fluttered in and out of the taller grasses. For everyone but Lowell, it was one of those peaceful moments you remember because of what comes afterward. What do they call it—the calm before the storm?

I was standing with the running hose in my hand, rinsing fresh water down Hannah's legs. I had my eye directly on JP, who was in constant motion—shaking his head around and making small jumps from side to side. He started to buck, hopping from rear to front legs, just as I had seen him do many times before, but what happened next was unexpected. First JP kicked back into a piece of rotten fence, which fell down with a loud clatter. Then the falling fence flushed out a rabbit that had been nesting in the weeds by the rail. The rabbit darted out in front of Buster, Mr. McCann's old retriever, who took off to chase it. With a panicked look in his eyes, JP bolted after Buster.

The foal's herding instinct had kicked in, but he was following the wrong leader. I watched as he sped on his long legs across the line where the fence was down along the road. He dashed across the road and into a meadow with some dark cedars on the far side. I could hear Buster's yelps as he made for the rabbit.

Hannah squealed and whinnied.

"JP!" I shouted.

Lowell jumped away from the wire and started to run down the road.

"April, he's too fast, I'm gonna lose them," he yelled. "Get on Rainy Day!"

"Come back and hold Hannah," I called. Lowell doubled back and ran over to where I stood with the rearing mare. "Take her in the barn. I'll go after JP. Call Marty if I'm not back in an hour. Number's on the fridge in the kitchen."

I ran over to Rainy Day and, hanging on to his mane, hoisted myself onto his bare back. I had never ridden him or any other horse without a saddle, but there was no time to think about that. I leaned forward and felt for his halter, which I grabbed with both hands on either side of his ears.

"Let's go, Rainy Day." I clucked him forward and pressed my heels into his sides.

Rainy Day leaped over the narrow roadside ditch and thundered down the dirt road. I saw where Buster and JP had passed into the woods, but I didn't think Rainy Day and I could follow them there.

"Whoa," I said as loudly as I could, and we halted.

I could barely make out the faint barking of Buster. A million terrible thoughts crossed my mind. JP could be bitten by a snake. He could trip and fall. He could get mangled by a barbed-wire fence. The only good thing was that he had headed away from Plattsburgh, where at least he wouldn't get caught in any traffic. No doubt he was following Buster along a deer path in the woods. Personally, I had never been farther on Boone's Passage than Mr. McCann's place and had no idea what lay ahead. Then I noticed that the road curved around, and that if I stayed on it I might catch up with Buster and JP when they popped out on the other side of the woods.

"Come on, Rainy Day," I urged.

He galloped along the road and I hung on for dear life. I tried to keep track of the woods on my right, and where we were in relation to where I had last seen JP. The wind and thumping sounds of Rainy Day's galloping hooves rushed into my ears. Something sharp—I assumed it was a pebble— kicked up in the rush. It hit me on the forehead, but there was no way I was going to let go of Rainy Day's halter to feel if I was bleeding. We came to a fork in the road and, again, I had no idea what to do. The county sign said Cedar Falls Road was to the right, which seemed the correct direction, but I wasn't sure. Cedar Falls Road was a very small gravel-and-dirt road, almost completely sheltered and shadowed by overhanging tree limbs. Boone's Passage was much more open and went off to the left, following the power line. I leaned forward and whispered in Rainy Day's right ear.

"You know what we're trying to do. Which way is JP? Where's the foal, boy?"

I made my hands as neutral as I could on his neck and waited. Rainy Day shook his head and took off on Cedar Falls Road.

It seemed like we rode for at least two miles, but the road had steep curves so maybe it wasn't that far after all. Eventually Cedar Falls Road opened up to meadows on either side of us. Rainy Day slowed to a trot and blew out air through his lips. I strained my ears but couldn't hear a thing. Not a bark. Not a leaf crunching. Nothing but the sound of us panting and the clomping of hooves on the unpaved road. I scanned the fields on either side of us but saw nothing except butterflies, birds, and a few turkey vultures spiraling up in the sky, scanning for small game.

We walked past the meadows until we were surrounded again by tall leafy trees. Judging by the distance, I figured we must have been at least one or two farms past Mr. McCann's. We were way off Boone's Passage and very far from Hannah. I didn't want to think about what would happen if JP got hurt or lost. I needed to focus on finding him and bringing him home safely.

I had to trust Rainy Day to find JP.

Up ahead I saw a break in the woods to our right. Rainy Day turned to go down the narrow country drive. There were two parallel ruts for wheels and a mound of weeds and dirt running down the center of the road. Rainy Day stayed in the right-hand track and slowed to a walk. About one hundred yards in, the drive opened up and what I saw next made me feel like we had ridden through a time machine.

Heading straight for us was a spry, glossy horse pulling a little square-topped black buggy. The horse, a dark bay, wore a simple black leather bridle and lifted his forelegs sharply. He held his head high. Even though he wore blinders I could see his bright eyes making contact with us. Rainy Day lowered his head in greeting. We slowed down as we approached one another, and I noticed that the driver of the buggy was a woman in a dark blue dress. She wore a white hat—a bonnet—that sat on the back of her head. The ties dangled down on her chest and ended in a loose knot. The bonnet didn't cover the front of her hair, which was brushed smoothly back and parted in the middle. She sat straight up on the bench, and a little boy in a straw hat sat beside her. He seemed to be about three or four years old, and wore a light blue shirt and dark suspenders. As we got closer, he leaned into her side. The woman lifted one hand from her reins and raised two fingers. I led Rainy Day off the driveway, smiled, and waved as she approached.

"Excuse me," I said as she pulled by us. I felt like I was speaking to a person from another era. "Hi. You haven't seen a little dark brown foal running through here, have you?"

The little boy shrank back as if I were a ghost. The woman stopped her horse. She appeared friendly but distant and cool. Almost unconsciously, I sat up a little taller in my saddle.

"A foal? No, I'm afraid not. But go on and ask my husband if you can find him. Straight on. Good luck."

"Thank you."

She lifted and dropped the reins, and her horse resumed walking. The buggy rattled by, and I let it get clear before nudging Rainy Day out of the weeds and back into the driveway.

Rolling along on big steel-rimmed wheels, the buggy was really just a plain black box except for a triangular orange sign stuck right in the middle of the rear end. I kept watching and saw the little boy lean out from the side and look back at me. Then he quickly pulled himself out of sight.

Up ahead I saw a farmhouse and a barn. Near the house was a laundry line with a row of dark blue dresses hanging still in the sunshine. Beside them dangled a row of black pants and white shirts. Not a ripple of wind stirred them.

Where in the world were we?

Before I had a chance to figure it out, I saw a small brown shape dash out from a hedgerow. Rainy Day nickered and shook his head, as if to get me to look in that direction.

"Buster!" I yelled. "Where's JP?"

Buster heard me and came running over. His frothing tongue lolled out of his mouth as he gasped for air. I jumped off Rainy Day and walked toward the barn ahead, leading him by the halter. I figured I could find a piece of rope to tie him up safely. Buster was leaping around my legs and sniffing at the new territory. "I hope this won't take long," I said to Rainy Day, turning toward the dark opening of the barn.

"Hello?" I called.

A tall man came out of the barn, wiping his hands on the sides of his pants. "Hello there."

"Excuse me for dropping in like this. My name is April and I'm looking for—"

For a second, I was distracted by the man's outfit. Like the little boy in the buggy, he was wearing a straw hat. He wore a white shirt and black pants, which were held up by plain black suspenders. He had a dark beard all around his chin but no mustache.

"—for a little foal that got scared and ran away. This dog belongs to a friend—I mean it's a man who just died, but it's his son's now, I guess."

The man took out a handkerchief and wiped his hands front and back, which were smudged with something black.

"Grease from cleaning tools," he explained. "Sorry. Are you talking about Joe McCann? Saw it in the paper. I'm sorry."

I wasn't sure what to say, so I nodded. Luckily, just at that moment Buster ran off toward the tree line. He yelped a high-pitched bark. I peered into the grass and thought I saw a little smudge of dark brown.

"I think that might be JP over there," I said. "He's not even a week old. I don't know how we can catch him."

"He'll be tired out, I imagine," the man said. "Shouldn't be too hard to bring him in. I'm John Rhinestat." He smiled and walked toward JP. "You can tie your horse to that post there and he'll be fine."

I walked with Rainy Day over to the hitching rail and found a piece of rope dangling on the ground. I tied him up as best I could and told him to stay put.

"I'll bring you some water in a sec, boy."

Then I turned and ran toward Mr. Rhinestat. His boots crunched through the tall grass of the field.

"We're haying next week," he explained. "Sorry you have to walk through this."

"No problem," I said, stomping down the tall, itchy grass that forced me to slow down in spite of my hurry and anxiety. "I just hope he's okay."

"Well, now," Mr. Rhinestat said, looking down into the grass. "Who've we got lying here, looking so lonesome?" He bent over and smiled.

"JP!" I cried, approaching the tiny and exhausted foal. He was lying on his side, breathing hard. When he heard my voice he lifted his head and looked up at me with a frightened but curious expression in his eyes. I lay down beside him and stretched my arm across his back, patting him all over. "You have no idea where you are, either, do you, little guy?" I murmured in his ear.

"I don't think he can take another step," I said, as if talking to myself. "What do I do? How will I get him home?"

I looked up at the man standing over us. "Do you have a horse trailer? Or maybe I could call Marty and he could bring his over."

Mr. Rhinestat looked puzzled. "It's April, you said, right?"

"Yes, sir. April Helmbach," I confirmed. JP was nuzzling under my arm and trying to nibble on my sleeve.

"Well, April, I guess I should tell you that we don't have a trailer here. Or a car, or a tractor with a motor, or a phone, or anything like that. We're Old Order Amish."

In all the commotion I had forgotten about the existence of this community, which everyone knew about but hardly ever saw. They shopped in a neighboring town, and otherwise kept mostly to themselves.

"That's our religion, so to speak," Mr. Rhinestat said. "But it's also our way of life. We choose to live and farm without what you would call modern-day conveniences."

I remembered the buggy that passed me on the drive into the farm.

"I guess I was more distracted than I thought," I said. "My stupid first thought was that you were reenactors."

Mr. Rhinestat looked like he might actually laugh out loud, but he held himself in check.

"I suppose that's the price we pay for keeping to ourselves," he said. "The English don't generally know what we're about, and if they do, they forget we're even here."

"Actually, I'm not English," I said. "I'm American. Some of my family came over from Germany, but others came from Ireland and France. So I guess I'm pretty much your average American mixture."

Mr. Rhinestat nodded at what I figured was a decent explanation of my heritage. We had done a project on immigration in seventh grade, and my teacher said over and over again that "America is a nation of immigrants and refugees."

"English is just what we call anyone who's not Amish," he said simply. He squatted down next to me as I patted JP. He opened the foal's lips and examined her tongue.

I wanted to say that it seemed a little drastic to lump everyone not like you into the same category, especially when that category didn't even describe what the other people were. How could someone who wasn't English be called English? But I didn't want to be rude.

"Do you have any way of contacting anyone in emergencies?"

As soon as I looked up at Mr. Rhinestat's face, I knew what the answer would be.

He shook his head. "Some families do, but we don't. All this youngster needs is water," he said. "Stay with him, and I'll be right back."

Mr. Rhinestat rose slowly to his full height and walked in big long steps back to the barn. He came back a few minutes later with a pan of cool water. He set it down in front of JP, who took a long drink, paused, then started lapping water again.

"I took the liberty of watering your gelding over there, too," Mr. Rhinestat said. "Nice manners, he has. Looks like he got beat up in a fight, though."

"That's Rainy Day," I said. "Those scars aren't from a fight. Did you hear about the accident on I-54 back in May?"

"That was the truck hauling all those horses to the slaughterhouse, no?" he asked, raising his eyebrows.

"Yeah. Rainy Day was in that trailer and I was there when it happened. My aunt and I got out to see if we could help, and Rainy Day found me in the middle of the scene. His face was bloody and he was limping a little. I adopted him a week later."

"You live in Plattsburgh?" he asked.

"I do."

JP sneezed and shook his head from side to side as if he had surprised himself.

Mr. Rhinestat slapped his hands on the tops of his thighs and said, "Let's go, then."

He squatted beside JP, facing in the same direction as the foal, and put his arms around JP's waist.

"Let's go, little man," he said. "Up with you now. Get back on those legs if you can."

JP wobbled a little on his long legs, but eventually got himself into a standing position. Mr. Rhinestat supported him firmly.

"No halter?" he said.

"He didn't have it on when he ran off," I said. "It's not the easiest thing in the world getting him to wear it."

Mr. Rhinestat let that go without comment.

"He's not weaned yet, so we cannot give him a treat. He is just going to have to come along because he wants to or because someone bigger wants him to. Go over and get that horse of yours. Take your time, this little guy is in no hurry."

No hurry was right. Nothing seemed to be in a hurry around the Rhinestat farm. There were no cars, no trucks, and no tractors to move people faster than a horse could go. There was no telephone ringing with news to get people all riled up about what other people were doing. Without the machines that make us move fast, it was easier for me to slow down. I took a deep breath, realized everything was going to be okay, and walked slowly through the tall grass over to Rainy Day. Things had been happening so quickly in the last week that I hadn't had the kind of leisurely time with Rainy Day that he and I had gotten used to in May, June, and the early weeks of July.

First Hannah needed extra attention, then the foal was born, and finally the sadness and social activity around Mr. McCann's death and funeral had colored the last several days. Only now did I realize that I missed those long stretches when Rainy Day was the only horse in my life, when I had nothing else to do but putter around in his barn—straightening tack, brushing off the saddle blanket, and organizing records and notes in the journal I was keeping.

Rainy Day stood placidly at the hitching rail, looking straight ahead. At the sound of my step, he turned as much as he could to watch me approach. I cupped his whiskery chin in my hand and looked deep into his eyes one after the other.

"You like it here, don't you?"

Keeping my hands on his chin, I imagined a younger, unscarred Rainy Day standing in a field of blue-green grass still wet with morning dew even though the sun was halfway up in the sky. Rainy Day was nibbling through the grass happily. The trees circled the pasture in wide canopies that made huge pools of shade. Rainy Day stopped tearing up grass and walked over to his mother or, as Marty would make me say, his dam. She rubbed her nose across his smooth colt's back and they stood together for some time.

I patted him all over his face and around his ear. "I guess I'll never know how you got from there to here, will I, boy?"

Leaving the rope knotted to his halter, I began untying the other end of the rope hitched to the rail.

"Come on, boy," I coaxed. "Let's go help JP."

We turned and walked back to where Mr. Rhinestat waited in the grass. He was speaking quietly and comfortingly to the foal, as if they had all the time in the world. JP tried to rear as Rainy Day got close, but Mr. Rhinestat shushed him back down. We let the two animals stand near each other for a few minutes so that JP could pattern his behavior to Rainy Day's.

"If we do this right," Mr. Rhinestat said, "we ought to be able to get JP here to walk alongside Rainy Day back to the barn to rest. All he needs is someone to follow."

"But what about getting them home?" I asked, concerned.

"One thing at a time, April."

I clucked Rainy Day forward at a snail's pace, praying JP would stick close. With Mr. Rhinestat pressing on his other side, he did just that, walking alongside Rainy Day. Our foursome advanced toward the open doors of the big white barn like the first row of a marching band.

As we passed the farmhouse, a plain white two-story wooden home with simple windows and a peaked roof, I noticed a little girl around eight standing in the doorframe. She had no expression on her face as she watched us move along. We were going so slowly that I got a good look at her outfit: a dark blue dress and white bonnet, almost exactly like the woman in the buggy. The little girl was barefoot. She stood with one foot resting on top of the other. Although she didn't wave or smile, something told me it was okay to do both.

Only then did she break into a grin.

The little girl's name was Esther and she was Mr. Rhinestat's daughter—*one* of Mr. Rhinestat's daughters. He and his wife had six kids, four boys and two girls. The oldest was Ammann, and he was my age, thirteen; the youngest was only a year old. His name was Dirk. The little boy I had seen in the buggy was Will. Esther said he was three and a half.

"That's four of you—Esther, Will, Ammann, and Dirk," I said. "Who am I missing?"

Esther looked at her father before replying. "There's my sister, Rachel," she said, sitting down next to me. "She's seven. And then there's Luther, my brother. He's six."

We were sitting in the Rhinestats' kitchen, drinking cold lemonade. After we settled Rainy Day and JP in a cool stall to rest, with big draft horses in stalls on either side, Mr. Rhinestat had invited me in. He told Esther to pour us all a drink, which she did without a word. She handed her father a glass, then poured another one for me. I could tell she was happy to have my company. Her eyes were big and open, and watching my every move.

I smiled and said thank you, and she smiled back shyly. The funny thing was, while she looked at me, I was having a hard time not staring at *her*. Esther's blond hair was parted in the middle and brushed smoothly back under her bonnet. It had been rolled and twisted back all around the hairline so not even a stray hair would come loose and fall into her face. How different my unruly hair must have looked to her. It was dark, wavy, and frizzy in the humidity, and barely held together in a low bun at the back of my head. I could feel that sweat and dust had glued single strands of hair to my cheeks. That happened whenever I rode hard. Instinctively I pushed the loose strands off my face and tucked them behind my ears. When I was younger, Aunt Patti used to tell me to go clean my room. "By the time you're done I want to see it neat as a pin," she would say. Looking at Esther, I kept hearing that phrase in my head. She was neat as a pin. From what I could see, the whole Rhinestat house was, too.

"So Ammann just finished seventh grade, then?" I asked. "Like me?"

"Eighth grade," Mr. Rhinestat said.

"Where does he go to school?" I asked.

"We have our own school—an Amish one not too far

from here," Mr. Rhinestat said. "We educate our children to our own ways. They all attend school together."

"Ammann is done with school now," Esther piped in. "Now he'll work with Papa on the farm all the time." She was kneeling on her chair, her legs tucked out of sight beneath her long dress.

I looked at Mr. Rhinestat as if to ask whether this was possible.

He didn't say anything, so I figured it was true. Still, I couldn't imagine being done with school after eighth grade. I couldn't wait to tell Lowell about these people. I was sure he would want to convert on the spot if it meant quitting school after one more year.

"Where's everyone else?" I asked.

"You passed my wife on her way to pay visits. The other children are with cousins. Esther stayed home to keep me company. After church this morning, I needed to see to one of our plow horses, which I was doing when you arrived. It's rare for an English person to drop by."

"Mr. Rhinestat, where exactly do the Amish come from that makes you say people are either Amish or English?"

I worried that this might sound too blunt, but it did annoy me just a little to be referred to as English.

"We're Christians," he said. "And we trace our heritage

back to a particular branch of Christians known as the Anabaptists."

"Tons of people out here are Baptists," I said. There were more Baptist churches in Plattsburgh than I could count. Most of my classmates went to one or another of the Southern Baptist churches around town. A few were Lutheran.

"You probably know this," Mr. Rhinestat said. "But as soon as Martin Luther in Europe led the break from the Roman church, many non-Catholic beliefs erupted. Anabaptists broke away from the mainstream Protestants in the 1500s. They thought a person had to make his own decision about whether to be a baptized Christian or not."

"I'm not sure what that means," I said.

"It means they didn't baptize babies. With all due respect, April," Mr. Rhinestat said with a smile, "we believe that only a fully mature adult has the wisdom to make a choice about something as important as adhering to the Word of God as revealed in the Bible. You could describe it this way—our church is voluntary, adult, holy, full-time, forgiving, caring, and disciplined. Some Anabaptists were known as Mennonites, nicknamed for one of their leaders at the time."

"I've heard of Mennonites," I said, taking a gingerbread

cookie off a plate Esther pushed toward me.

"In the early years the Anabaptists were martyred for their beliefs. Many of us were thrown into the river and drowned. We tell a story about a Dutch Anabaptist, Dirk Willems. In 1569, he was being chased across a frozen lake by the local sheriff when the sheriff plunged through the ice and was about to sink. Willems turned back and helped the sheriff to safety. Back in town, the sheriff had him arrested and burned at the stake."

Esther was nibbling a cookie into a crescent moon but I could tell she was paying close attention. No doubt she had heard these stories over and over, but she still seemed to hang on every word. It reminded me of that day when Mr. McCann talked about the Civil War periods in Plattsburgh. Then I had been impatient to get going, but today I resolved to sit through this history lesson.

"Eventually, a man from Switzerland—Jacob Ammann—wanted to make some changes in the way he practiced his faith. Since his time, which was around 1700, his followers have been called the Amish."

"Amish, not Ammannish," Esther said. She had finished her cookie and was now stirring the sugar that had settled on the bottom of her lemonade. She lifted up the soggy granules and sucked them off her spoon.

Listening to Mr. Rhinestat, I couldn't believe how he was talking about things that had happened more than three hundred years ago as if they had happened yesterday.

"As you can see," he continued, "we tend to hold to our customs. We try to live the Word simply and put it into practice in our daily lives with humility. We dress in plain clothes. Our women do not wear jewelry—not even wedding rings. We teach our children that working hard and exercising discipline are the way we show our devotion to God."

I got the feeling that Mr. Rhinestat was telling me all this almost as a way of reminding Esther. He was looking as much at her as he was at me. She was still playing with her spoon, digging out the last bits of sugar, but she had settled down in her chair and listened to her dad.

"When did the Mennonites and Amish come here?" I asked.

"'Here' as in America or 'here' as in Plattsburgh?"

"Both, I guess."

"Well, the Amish came over from Europe in the early 1700s during Colonial times. We settled mostly in southern Pennsylvania and continued to speak German. In fact, we all speak a dialect of German at home to this day. It's the first language our children learn, their mother tongue, you might say. In the 1800s, many Amish folk migrated west—

just like the other pioneers—to Ohio, Indiana, Iowa, and parts of Canada. Some families settled in Missouri about fifty years ago. There are only a few dozen families around this part of the county. All we need is fertile land and privacy. We have one another, and we have our faith."

He swallowed the last sip of his lemonade. Responding to one glance from her father, Esther cleared the three glasses, took them to the sink, washed them all by hand, and set them in the drying rack. In some ways, it was just like what I did every day after lunch. I, too, was responsible for getting my dishes clean for the next meal. But in another way, it couldn't be more different. I threw all my dishes in a machine, which was connected to electrical power, which cleaned the dishes for me so I could go do something else that probably required electricity—like watch TV.

It seemed impossible to believe that people could live this way in our day and age. Yet it also seemed kind of nice to have everything all figured out and someone in charge telling you what to do. In a way, I was envious. Whenever I was about to hang out with friends, Aunt Patti always reminded me to "make good choices." I knew she meant for me to be responsible and not get into trouble with all the things kids get into trouble with. But now I wondered what it would be like not having to make the hard choices in the first place.

Wouldn't that remove the cause of the pressure? I knew I should have been trying to figure out how to get myself and the horses back, but I wasn't quite ready to leave.

"You make it sound so perfect," I said. At the risk of offending him, I asked, "Do you guys have any problems?"

Mr. Rhinestat chuckled quietly. Everything about him was contained and mild. He stood up and put his hand on Esther's shoulder.

"Go on out and bring in the wash," he said. I supposed he didn't want to talk about problems in front of her.

"Come back to the barn with me, April. Let's go check on the horses." We passed back into the heat of the day. The sudden glare of the sun made me sneeze after being in the cool darkness of the house.

"Gesundheit," Mr. Rhinestat said.

We crunched over gravel toward the barn. Not far away, I saw Esther reaching up and pulling the plain dark pants and dresses off the line. She had to stand on the tip of her bare toes to reach. Then she dropped the clothes in one basket and stuck the clothespins into a little fabric pouch that was tied around her waist.

"Part of being humble is accepting our flaws and weaknesses," Mr. Rhinestat said as we walked. "We make mistakes. We lose our temper. Sometimes the weather doesn't cooperate with our plans and plants. People get sick. People get jealous, or behave unkindly in some other way. The thing is, we consider our community a single organism. If one part of us has a problem, we work together to heal it. And of course we have customs for dealing with particular problems."

I was curious about what those customs might be, but now I was distracted by Rainy Day, who was leaning over the half-wall of the stall to exchange greetings with an enormous draft horse. The powerful workhorse was a palomino, a beautiful golden color with a cream-colored tail and mane. He had white socks on his hind legs and a long white marking down the middle of his face.

"We call him Gunther," Mr. Rhinestat said, giving the big horse a rub. "He's the guy who wasn't feeling too well this morning. I put some extra alfalfa in his feed and gave him a rest, and he seems like he feels better now. Looks like he likes the company."

"Hey, Gunther," I said. "What do you do around here?"

"Gunther and his partner here pull the plow. We've got our tractor modified so they can pull that, too."

"So the buggy horses only pull buggies and these horses only do the harder work."

"Exactly," Mr. Rhinestat confirmed.

We watched the horses for a moment or two.

"You know, April," Mr. Rhinestat said, "It's interesting that you ended up here today. I might even say it's a case of divine intervention."

"That makes me a little nervous."

Mr. Rhinestat laughed and went on to explain that several disturbing things had been happening between the local Amish community and the county government. For years, he said, they had been farming their land, raising their children, observing their customs, and all in all living peacefully and invisibly on the outskirts of town. Just like the Amish in other parts of the country, they paid taxes even though they didn't use the services the taxes paid for, like public schools, police, Social Security, and that kind of thing.

"We know that a lot of those tax dollars we pay the federal government are paying for the war," he said. "And while we object to war, we don't hold back even on that tax."

"So what's the problem?" I asked.

"Well, I'm not too sure, April. Maybe you can help me understand."

He went on to explain that some new county commissioner in Plattsburgh seemed to be trying to change things for the Amish. She wanted to levy a special buggy tax, claiming that the steel wheels of their buggies make the county roads—the gravel ones especially—more expensive to maintain.

"Now she wants access to my land. Says the county needs to make a deal with a cell phone company to put up a transmitting tower. I've got a rise over on the other side of my property that's pretty high. You can see for miles." Mr. Rhinestat pointed off into the distance, where the rolling Ozarks melted into a haze of pollen and dust. "Anyway, she's trying to say the county has a legal right to this land for the greater good of the community."

"Who's this she?" I asked.

"Oh, her name's in the paper all the time. What was it again?"

Mr. Rhinestat filled a bucket with water and hung it on a rack in the stall. I watched JP reach around with his head towards a fly on his back end, but his neck wasn't long enough.

"Follette," he said. "Barbara Follette."

I didn't recognize the name, but I repeated it under my breath so I could remember to ask Aunt Patti about her when I got home.

Home! I had lost all track of time.

"Mr. Rhinestat, I really need to get back. I'm sure Hannah, JP's mother, is a wreck, and people are probably worried about me."

Mr. Rhinestat looked at JP.

"Let's get a halter on him. I've got a spare you can return some other time." Mr. Rhinestat took a small fleece-lined halter from a peg on the barn wall. "There. He ought to be fine walking if you take it slow and keep him walking right next to you and Rainy Day, the same way we did getting in here."

Before leaving, I asked if I could go say good-bye to Esther. I found her inside, folding the clothes on top of a plain wooden table. Her face lit up when I walked in, and she laid a perfectly folded white shirt down on top of a pile of exactly identical shirts. Then she asked me if I wanted to see the doll she had made. The doll was cloth, stuffed full so that it held its shape.

"Her name's Carol Anne Jane Elizabeth Mary," Esther said.

"Carol Anne Jane Elizabeth Mary," I repeated, laughing. "Whoa. That's a lot of names."

"I couldn't decide which I liked best, so I just named her all of them. Will you ever come back here again?" she asked.

Esther seemed to switch from miniature grown-up to little kid so quickly—one minute folding laundry and the next playing with a doll. I definitely was done playing with dolls by the time I was ten. Actually, I think I tossed aside my last doll when I was six.

"Sure, if I'm invited." I smiled.

Esther beamed at that. "Wait here," she said.

She disappeared into the shadows of the pantry and returned with a small loaf of bread and a jar of jam.

"Mama and I made this yesterday," she said. "Here's a bag I made that you can put it in."

Like a little shopkeeper, Esther put the gifts in a small tote sewn together out of what looked like an old cotton T-shirt.

"Thank you so much," I said.

"Listen," Mr. Rhinestat said. "I'd be grateful to hear how this foal is doing. That is, if you ever find yourself out this way again."

"Well, I've got this halter to return to you, Mr. Rhinestat. And there's Carol Anne Jane Elizabeth Mary to see again," I joked.

Mr. Rhinestat smiled, and I set off for the long walk back to the McCann place, Buster walking in front of me as I lead Rainy Day and JP. My invitation to return confirmed, I hoped that next time I would be able to go for a ride in that buggy.

"I'm really sorry about the fence," Nelson said at dinner that night. "If Pop had the place in shape, JP never would have been able to run off."

Lowell, Aunt Patti, and I were all twirling spaghetti and slurping noisily. Chase lay across Lowell's feet under the table. Spaghetti was the one meal Lowell couldn't really sneak down to him, which must have driven Chase crazy.

"These tomatoes are fantastic, Patti," Nelson said, spearing a fat golden yellow chunk of tomato and looking at it on the end of his fork.

"They are good, aren't they?" she said. "I wonder if I can grow them a little smaller and meatier."

Aunt Patti was definitely not modest about her vegetable garden. She grew all of our herbs and most of the vegetables we ate throughout the summer. One thing she especially liked about having Rainy Day was using his droppings as fertilizer. He probably made enough to fertilize an entire farm. What she didn't use, Marty came and shoveled up to take over to his stable for composting.

The group dinner had materialized out of the drama of the day. I came back to the modern world to find everyone working the phones trying to find me, and we spent most of the afternoon talking about the Rhinestats—the hand washing, the old-fashioned clothes, the kindness of Mr. Rhinestat, the buggy, and the huge draft horses.

We all got up to clear our plates, but Nelson stayed by the sink to rinse them off and put them in the dishwasher. Lowell took the dampened rag Nelson passed him and went back to clean the Parmesan bits off the table. It occurred to me that if we had been Amish, only Aunt Patti and I would have been doing this kitchen work. Nelson and Lowell would have just left the room.

As it was, Aunt Patti and I were the ones to walk away from the dinner chores. We went into the living room and plopped down on the couch. Aunt Patti got her scrapbooking stuff out from under the coffee table and started leafing through some old magazines. A couple of weeks ago she had finished her mimesis project, which was about plants and insects that appear to be dangerous or poisonous to confuse predators. Nature's copycats, she called them. "Nothing wrong with appearances being deceiving," she said.

In addition to gardening, scrapbooking was one of

Aunt Patti's hobbies. She enjoyed the whole process—first cutting pictures out of nature magazines, then typing up descriptions, printing out scientific studies, and gluing all of this information into huge books, which had black pages and thick leather covers. Most of her scrapbooks had something to do with nature. Privately, I believed her fantasy was that one day she would be a teacher and use these books as classroom resources. There was an entire row of her projects lined up on the bottom shelf of one of our bookcases.

Nelson and Lowell came out from the kitchen and joined us. Lowell flipped on the TV and started channel surfing.

"So what's the next topic?" Nelson said, watching Aunt Patti open up an old nature magazine. In the last week he had been hanging around our place more and more.

She tossed down the magazine and sighed.

"I'm too distracted to start something now," she said. "I got a call a couple of days ago to do the flowers for a huge wedding at the end of the summer."

Lowell caught my eye and pointed to his watch. We were going to meet some friends for a movie, and I knew he was concerned about being on time. I nodded and went over to the door to get my shoes on.

"That's great," Nelson said to Aunt Patti.

"Yes and no. I've heard the bride's mother has kind of a reputation."

"Who is it?" Nelson asked.

"Barbara Follette. She's on the town council or some other local government body."

"No way," I said, and Nelson and Aunt Patti turned to me. "Mr. Rhinestat said something about her to me today. I meant to talk to you about it. The county commissioner, right?"

"Yeah. What a strange coincidence. How would the county commissioner know Mr. Rhinestat?" Aunt Patti asked.

"He said she's trying to do a bunch of stuff that the Amish families are not happy about," I explained. "It's a long story. Can you still drive us over to the mall?"

I could tell Aunt Patti wasn't really listening to that last reminder because she went right on talking. "Well, I don't know about what she's trying to do to the Amish families, but I do know that she and her family have been major landowners here forever. My friend Sarah works at the salon where Mrs. Follette gets her hair done. She says that Mrs. Follette is mean and nasty to everyone. Not a nice person."

"That sounds like good old gossip," Nelson said. "One of the things that drove me away from here. Everyone yakking about everyone else." He sat beside Lowell and watched the stations flash by. When he caught a glimpse of a cop-and-court show, he told Lowell to stop flipping. Clearly, he was not pleased at the turn of the conversation, and Lowell was jerking his knee up and down, anxious to leave. I glanced at the kitchen clock. We had plenty of time.

"I know it's stupid gossip," Aunt Patti admitted. "But what can I do? I have to work for her. You don't know how miserable it can be to work for a jerk. "

"Actually, Patti, maybe I do," Nelson said seriously, in a tone I had never heard him use before. "But you took the job, right?"

"Yeah," Aunt Patti said.

"Well," he went on, "you didn't let the gossip stop you from doing business with her."

"No, I didn't," she agreed. "But I wonder if it's going to be more trouble than it's worth."

Aunt Patti looked at me as if she were waking up suddenly. "Wait, April, what did you say that Amish man told you about her? April? Where are you going?"

Now it was my turn to tune *her* out. I was on my way to the landing outside the kitchen door, where we piled our old newspapers. I had suddenly remembered the article about the buggy tax—the one I never finished reading. It had dawned on me that this must be the same story Mr. Rhinestat had mentioned. So much had happened since I had given the newspaper a passing glance that it had slipped my mind. I dug under several days' worth of old papers until I found the one I was looking for. Finally I saw it, but this time with new eyes:

PROTESTERS VOW TO NIX "BUGGY TAX"

PLATTSBURGH—Several members of Plattsburgh's small and traditionally reclusive Amish community appeared before the county commissioner Monday night to register their objection to a proposed "buggy tax" on their horse-drawn carriages—their only means of transportation.

"We respect this nation's laws and participate responsibly as tax-paying citizens," said Martin Luerhmann, one of the elders of the community, when testifying before the commissioners. "But we believe this extra levy places an unfair burden on Amish families, whose tax dollars, by the way, already go toward the upkeep of schools, highways, and other public services that we do not use."

Commissioner Barbara Follette told Mr. Luerhmann that his objections had been duly noted and would be taken into consideration.

Follette later told the *Plattsburgh Sun* that she suspected it would be difficult to refrain from implementing the tax, given that the steel bands of the buggy wheels damaged the unpaved county roads far more than rubber tires do.

"It's clear that the county must find a way for those who choose to live by antiquated customs to pay their fair share, which is what this revenue plan is all about," Follette said.

In a related story, BeneTran Telephone, the Houston-based cellular telephone giant, has been negotiating with the county in order to place additional towers that might bring hitherto inaccessible regions into their network. The property of Amish elder John Rhinestat has been identified by BeneTran engineers as an ideal location. To date, Rhinestat has denied any and all access to his land to BeneTran representatives.

"This is the year 2007," Follette said. "It seems to be taking some people longer than others to come to terms with this fact."

Neither Mr. Luerhmann nor Mr. Rhinestat could be reached for comment on the cellular tower proposal.

I took the paper back inside and showed it to Aunt Patti. She read it and passed it to Nelson, who read the article from beginning to end.

"I wonder if it was people like this who drove Pop out of public service," he said.

"I wonder," Aunt Patti said, smiling at him grimly.

"We gotta go," I said. "Aunt Patti?"

Driving to the movie, I wasn't sure whose side I was on. It did seem strange for people to totally ignore the fact that everyone around them was acting one way while they acted another. Even if the Rhinestats' life was nice and peaceful, shouldn't they, and all the rest of the Amish, try harder to fit in with the rest of the world? So what if Barbara Follette was mean—it sounded like she was—but I wasn't sure that what she was doing was wrong. Everything that night—the mall, the candy, the movie, our friends—felt light-years away from what I had seen earlier that day.

"See you tomorrow," I said to Lowell after his mom brought us home.

"Yup. Bright and early," he said sarcastically, but I knew he loved working for Nelson. He liked having someplace to go, earning his own money, and making himself useful. It seemed like he looked stronger, older, and more confident every day.

I came in the back door and found Nelson and Aunt Patti sitting on the couch together watching an old romantic movie—*When Harry Met Sally*.

"Hey, I'm back," I said, letting them know I was home. Then I went out to the barn to check on Rainy Day.

It was a beautiful night, warm and buzzing with the sounds of summer. I heard a couple of motorcycles rev in the distance. On the small lane behind the barn, a bunch of kids laughed as they sped by on their bikes, racing home before it was completely dark. A dog barked and its owner hollered at it to come in and shut up. Typical sounds of a Plattsburgh summer night. Rainy Day's eyes were shining, and he nickered when I came in and took his chin in my hands.

"Hey, boy," I said.

I pulled the dangling string that turned on the bare light

bulb in the stall and blinked in the sudden brightness. I gathered the grooming supplies and carried them over to Rainy Day.

Even though I was tired, I took my time with every single step. First I put fresh oats mixed with some hay and corn into his feed bucket, so he'd have something to eat while I worked. He plunged in his muzzle and began crunching.

There was caked mud and dirt all up his legs, and his hooves were filled with little rocks and stones from our long outing. As I brushed and cleaned him all over, my thoughts were whirling from the day.

No doubt there were good and bad things about whatever day and age you lived in. In a way I felt sorry for Esther. There was so much she didn't get to do or see, things she probably didn't even know existed. Then again, she seemed so safe and content in her own family, always knowing exactly what her role was and what everyone in her community expected her to do. Then there was that boy-girl issue. Maybe it was because I had grown up with Aunt Patti, and it had always been just the two of us, but I didn't think I would like having to take orders from men just because I was a girl. And I was especially curious about her brother Ammann, the kid who was practically my age but already done with school. I wondered if I would ever get to meet him in person.

When I completed the chores, I turned off the light, sat down in the clean hay, leaned back against the wall, and kept Rainy Day company. I liked listening to him shift from one foot to the other and finish up the food in his bucket. I closed my eyes and imagined him in that blue-green grass again. This time he was rolling around on his back in a field still wet with morning dew. He was much smaller, not quite as small as JP, but still a colt for sure. Then I saw someone approach him with a halter, and he got up and raced away to the other side of the pasture at full gallop. I opened my eyes to the darkness of the barn.

I had known it wouldn't be easy training JP. Marty had warned me that even the best-natured horses put up a fight when they're first confronted with the halter, the rope, and the handling of their body. Still, I had not anticipated what kinds of things could go wrong if I didn't pay close enough attention every little second. Running away like that, JP was only doing what came naturally. Somehow, I would have to get him to accept what didn't come naturally. And like Marty said, it would be for his own good.

JP turned one month old in August. He had grown stronger on his legs and more confident around the paddock. His head and legs no longer looked so huge compared to his torso, and he grew more comfortable wandering away from Hannah. Every day, Marty made sure that I spent time working with the foal. The main task had been getting him used to the halter, which was never easy unless Hannah was standing right there next to us. Marty had confirmed what my book had stated—if I didn't get JP used to people handling his head, he might develop head shyness, which would make his life and his owner's life very unpleasant. Same thing with the rest of his body, but especially his legs and feet. Even if he didn't need any grooming, I made a point to rub each of his legs and handle each one of his hooves at least once every single day. I also made sure that JP was used to the look, feel, and smell of rope and leather straps, as well as all the tack and materials that eventually he would need to accept. Every so often the foal would try to kick me or nibble at my clothes. One

sharp "no" usually brought him right back under control.

"It's all in the associations," Marty had said during the first few weeks. "You can teach a horse to feel good about just about anything if he comes to associate that thing or activity with something pleasant."

"Like my third-grade teacher giving us lemon drops during standardized tests," I said. "I actually remember the taste and feel of those lemon drops more than I remember anything about the tests."

"That's exactly what I mean," Marty blurted. "JP here's too young for sweets, but gentle pats and rubs along with a nice tone of voice will do the trick. Same thing to make him stop a bad behavior. You want him to have an unpleasant feeling associated with behaviors you don't like."

Marty draped his arm around JP's back and put his cheek against the foal's head. "These guys are just little toddlers," he said. "Even a full-grown horse, they say, is no more intelligent than a kid."

"Gee, thanks, Marty."

"A young kid, I mean. Three or four years old. Truth is, April, they're creatures of habit. As herd animals, they come by it naturally. They behave the way they do because that's what they've always done. So our job is to make sure their habits are what we want in the first place. You get it?"

Actually, I did get it. "We don't want the horse to question why we're asking them to do anything. We just want them to do it."

"That's it," Marty said.

JP was a playful foal, romping next to Hannah as much as he could, but I could tell how much he had learned. When he saw me arrive in the morning, he would trot over to greet me with a exaggerated head shake. Then he would wait patiently while I unsaddled Rainy Day and set him loose to join Hannah in the pasture. Alone with JP, I would pat and rub him all around his body, especially his sides, which horses naturally want to defend. Once it was clear that he was submissive, I would tell him to run over and go play with the others.

JP and I weren't the only ones who developed a routine around the farm. Every day, Lowell got dropped off a couple of hours after I arrived. He and Nelson grew close, partly because they were working together on various projects around the house and farm, but also because Lowell could relate to Nelson better than he could to his own dad. Lowell's dad was nice, but I knew Lowell thought about things in a different way. Lowell didn't want to grow up and work in a factory or run big machines like his dad. He was genuinely interested in school and asked Nelson about college and being a lawyer. Once I overheard them talking about options.

"So when did you know that you wanted to be, or could be, a lawyer?" Lowell had asked.

"It sounds stupid, but I noticed that I always won arguments. With everyone—older siblings, parents, teachers, friends. It was my twelfth-grade history teacher who said I should think about being a lawyer. He was kind of joking, but that was the first I'd heard of it. In college I did debate club, and things just sort of developed from there."

Lowell and Nelson spent a lot of time filing the papers that had been stored in the attic. They came down for breaks marveling at how involved Mr. McCann had been in things like road design and grading, and even fire and sheriff's department decisions.

One day over ham sandwiches, Nelson said, "I had always thought of my dad as a 'man of the land,'" Nelson said. "By the time I came along, that's what he was. But I guess you never know about your parents, really. I mean about their lives before you come into them. Who knew he was a civic leader?"

"All I really know about my parents is their lives before I came along," I said, grabbing a handful of corn chips. "There was so little life for my parents after I was born. Everything that I know was told to me by other people—

Aunt Patti, Marty, my grandma."

"How old were you again, April? When they died?"

"Four."

Nelson shook his head. "That must have been tough," he said.

"I think it was," I said. "But as I get older I realize that my memories of them are practically nil. My real childhood memories are all with Aunt Patti. From time to time I get this dropping-away feeling, a little like the feeling you get in your stomach when you're swinging. It's an odd sensation, but it does remind me that a very large and intense thing happened when I was a kid. Does that make sense?"

"It does," Nelson said.

The days went by, and it sure didn't seem like Nelson was in a big hurry to go back to St. Louis. Aunt Patti had told me that Nelson had taken a leave of absence from work, that he had received quite a bit of life insurance money in addition to his share of the inheritance after Mr. McCann died. Nelson wanted to see the farm in tip-top shape before selling it. That's what he told Aunt Patti anyway. Personally, I had my suspicions about Nelson's reasons for staying on in Plattsburgh. He seemed to be getting very comfortable at our house, which I guess was fine to a certain extent, but really, I kind of liked things the way they were—just Aunt Patti and me.

One day, I brought up the subject directly. We were eating dinner alone for the first time in a while.

"So would all this time with Nelson qualify as you and him getting serious?"

"April," she said, laughing nervously. "Getting serious? That's the last thing I plan on doing. Do I like him and do I like spending time with him? Sure. Is it hard to meet guys living here? Yes. Beyond that, I don't know. His life's up in the air right now and mine is not. We'll see."

This seemed like an unsatisfying answer. "Aunt Patti," I said, pushing a little harder, "what I mean is, would you say that at this point you guys are going out?"

Aunt Patti put down her knife and fork. She looked at me and smiled. "Going out. Well now, I guess I would have to say yes, sort of, but only in the very earliest stage."

"Hmm," I said, taking a sip of milk. I wasn't sure what I thought about this, but I did feel better knowing how things stood.

The next morning I got to the farm around six-thirty AM, same as always, and was surprised that Marty had beaten me there. I found him in the barn measuring out six feet of rope.

"You remember what happens today?" he said.

"Not really." I may have been up and about at that hour

every single morning that summer, but that didn't mean my brain was totally awake. It was always closer to nine or ten before my mind caught up with what my body was doing.

"Today this boy starts learning to lead," Marty said.

"So what do we do?"

"Well, he got a little bit of a head start back when he ran off that day. He was led alongside Rainy Day, remember? Let's hope he remembers that today. We'll start him off walking next to Hannah, and then we'll coax him away to walk with you or me on his own," Marty explained, turning to the tack wall and exchanging the six-foot lead rope for a much longer one.

"I'm not going to take any chances," he said. "I don't want JP to be able to resist at all. He can't have any choice about whether or not to follow."

"How can you make sure about that?" I asked.

"We're going to loop the lead rope around his croup," Marty said, carrying the long rope over to JP.

"What will that do?"

"Think about it. If the rope's around both his back and front ends, any pull at this end will automatically force his hindquarters to move forward," Marty said. "He won't be able to plant his rear legs in protest. They'll move whether he wants them to or not. It's our way or the highway," he added, laughing.

While Marty arranged JP, I put Hannah into her halter and clipped on her lead rope.

It was easy at first. As soon as I moved Hannah out of her stall, Marty led JP beside her and we led them together into the corral outside the barn. Marty handed me Hannah's lead rope, and we walked along the metal borders of the corral, all three of us, for several minutes.

Then Marty came and took Hannah's lead from me. He quietly guided the mare in another direction, saying, "Okay, April, be gentle and coax him to come with you now."

"Let's you and me go this way, JP," I said, putting my face close by his head.

JP laid back his ears and rolled his eyes toward Hannah. Obviously, he was not pleased. He seemed confused, too. I could feel him start to pull against me toward Hannah. She simply followed Marty right toward the opening of the corral. Marty turned around and made Hannah stand still, facing us.

"Don't look at me, April. Keep talking to him and look where you want him to go. Stay right with his shoulder there. That's it," Marty said, quietly encouraging me.

I led JP in a slow circle along the rail, praising him when I felt him moving with me and not pulling away. The rope around his croup definitely helped. Only once did he try to rear, curling up his front legs in protest.

"Whoa, JP, get down now," I said, pulling the lead toward the ground. We walked steadily while I waited for the next set of instructions.

"Now turn him to your left and go straight," Marty said.

JP and I spent ten more minutes following Marty's commands. It took all my concentration to focus on moving in the right direction, turning when told, keeping my eyes ahead of me, and making sure JP stayed in step.

"Okay, then, April. We're gonna stop there. That's enough school for the first day. Bring him over here and we'll turn them out for the rest of the morning. Now he gets recess for the rest of the day."

JP was all done with school, and it wasn't even seven o'clock in the morning. Marty freed me to tend to old Moses and the other animals. I found the giant gray-and-pink hog lying on his side in his small section of the barn. He lifted his head when I entered, as if wondering what delicious scraps I might have in hand today. JP was going to have to be trained every single day and remember those lessons for the rest of his life. Old Moses had only one thing to learn: Humans brought food and scratched pigs behind their ears. For this pig, all of life is recess.

chapter

A few days later, while finishing the McCann chores, I noticed the little halter I had borrowed from Mr. Rhinestat hanging on a crooked nail in the barn. Seeing it reminded me that Mr. Rhinestat had asked for an update on JP, and that I had completely forgotten to pay a second visit. Back at the house, Nelson invited me to stay for lunch.

"Thanks, Nelson," I said, "but I've got plans this afternoon. I'll see you later on."

I saddled Rainy Day, and we rode out on Boone's Passage away from Plattsburgh. As long as I got back for the evening chores, I was free for the middle of the day.

Apart from being curious about the Rhinestats and wanting to see them again, I was looking forward to getting some distance from home. Aunt Patti was stressed about the Follette wedding. From what I gathered, Mrs. Follette had changed her mind about a couple of important things. In a matter of days, she had switched the groomsmen's flowers from red to white, rethought the look of the bridesmaids' bouquets, and booked three different places to have the party. As just one of the contractors for the wedding, Aunt Patti was sometimes the last to hear about these changes. Usually Aunt Patti was pretty flexible and patient with nervous hosts, but for some reason she was starting to take her stress out on me, picking on tiny things I did or didn't do. Why hadn't I vacuumed the living room? Couldn't I run to the store and get some eggs? Hadn't she said be home by nine o'clock? What was I thinking, putting an empty mustard jar back in the fridge? She always apologized afterwards and berated herself for being impatient, but it meant that unless she directly asked for my help, I was keeping to myself.

Trotting along Boone's Passage to Cedar Falls Road at a normal pace made me realize that we had gone pretty far the day JP had run away. Rainy Day seemed happy to be stretching his legs for the long ride. A high-stepping bounce in his gait told me he was feeling good.

I found the opening in the woods and turned down the drive. We slowed to a walk, in case any buggies or riders were coming the other way. As we came around a bend, and I saw the familiar hanging laundry and tidy outbuildings, I scanned the scene for signs of the family. Everything seemed quiet.

I rode up to the hitching rail in the barnyard and tied up Rainy Day.

"Let's see who's around," I said.

I walked to the back of the barn and looked out into the field beyond. A few hundred yards away, I saw a small dust cloud, in front of which were the two palomino draft horses. They were pulling a faded green wooden wagon filled to the brim with dry hay. Standing in the wagon were two people in blue shirts and straw hats. I figured they were Mr. Rhinestat and Ammann. They were too far away for me to call or wave, so I turned and went to the front screen door of the house and knocked on the frame.

"Hello?"

The woman who appeared on the other side of the screen was definitely Mrs. Rhinestat. I recognized her from the day she was driving the buggy. She was in the same long dark blue dress. She was barefoot and holding a round little boy on her hip. Her skin was smooth and pale, and her blondish hair was pulled tightly back until it disappeared into her white bonnet. Seeing me, the baby smiled, leaned into her chest and clamped on even tighter.

"Hi. I'm April Helmbach. The one who came by, looking for a foal that had run away?"

I wanted her to interrupt me, push open the screen door, and say, "Why, yes, of course, I remember you, come in, come in."

But she didn't.

She nodded and gave me a small smile. She shifted the baby higher on her hip and said, "John told me about that. I am glad you found him."

We stood there for a long awkward moment.

Behind her a shadow appeared. It was Esther, and she was holding her doll in one hand and some sort of can with a spout in the other.

"Hi, Esther! It's me, April. Is this your baby brother, Dirk?"

She moved close to her mother and said hi.

Mrs. Rhinestat looked down and put her hand on top of Esther's head. "Yes, this is Dirk. Esther, have you replenished all the lanterns on the windowsill?"

"Almost, Mama. But there is no more kerosene in here." She lifted up the can.

"I just stopped by to tell Mr. Rhinestat how JP is doing," I said. "He had asked for an update. I also wanted to thank you for the delicious oat bread and strawberry jam. Esther gave me a loaf and a jar to take home, and everyone loved it so much. It was all eaten up in one day."

"You are welcome," she said, relaxing a little. "John and Ammann will be back shortly. Esther, would you like to go out and play with April? I'll get more kerosene for you and finish what I was doing."

"Yes, Mama."

Esther came out and her baby brother leaned forward to come, too. Mrs. Rhinestat kept a tight grip on him, then turned back into the shadows of the house.

"I'll show you my pebble collection," she said, taking my hand.

Esther led me to a white playhouse in the backyard. The structure was so small, I had to duck my head to enter. There was a little square window in one wall, a plain table and chairs, and a small wooden cabinet with wooden knobs. I squashed myself into the tiny chair. Esther came in after me and sat down at the table. On the table she had arranged ten or twelve rows of small rocks and pebbles. Even though I felt like a giant in a mouse house, it was one of the coziest places I had ever seen.

"This is the house I share with Rachel," she said, setting her doll on her lap. "Papa built it for us when I was three. And these are my pebbles."

"Those are very nice," I said.

Esther reached under the table and brought up a tiny watering can. She poured water over all the pebbles so that they turned glossy and bright. The fragments of white and pink quartz shone, and the solid black rocks seemed like gems.

"I like to make them shine," she said. "They're prettier when they're wet. Would you like a cup of tea?"

I sat up straight to get into the game. "Yes, thank you."

Esther smiled at my formal "playing tea party" voice.

It had been a long time since I had pretended to be someone else. Lowell and I had always played when we were little, usually on the rusty old play set in his backyard. Our games were mostly wild escapes from dangerous creatures or bad guys.

Esther opened the little cabinet and took out two miniature china teacups and saucers and a teapot. She poured water from her watering can into the teapot and then put it back under the table.

"How do you do?" she said, and I could tell this was the official start of the tea party.

"Very well, thank you. How do you do?"

With a certain formality, Esther poured out two cups of water-tea. Then she picked up her cup, stuck out her pinky, and took a pretend sip. I did the same.

"Quite delicious," I said. "Whatever kind of tea is this?"

"It's a combination of sassafras and hollyhock leaves," she said. "But I always add a spot of gingermint leaves, too."

It was hard not to laugh. We went on playing a while longer, until I heard the sound of approaching horses.

Esther broke from her accent and put all the tea things away. She poured more water all over her pebbles and we came out of the playhouse.

I followed her to the barn. She ran up to one of the horses and cuddled his head. I waved to Mr. Rhinestat and he nodded in reply. He hopped off the wagon and led the horses to the hitching post to get them out of their harnesses. Ammann was still standing inside with a pitchfork in his hand.

"Hi!" I said. "I'm April Helmbach."

"Ammann," the boy said.

"April," Mr. Rhinestat said. "Let us get this hay unloaded and turn out the horses. We'll be right with you."

"Sure. Anything I can do to help?" I offered.

"Sure there is. Help me with the tack and it'll go faster. Ammann, show April how we keep it. And make sure there's fresh water in their buckets. Esther, go tell Mama to set a place for April at lunch."

The time I entered the barn with JP, I had been concerned about keeping close to him and hadn't really paid any attention to the space. Today I was amazed at the inside of this barn, which was so different from Marty's, or the McCanns', or even Rainy Day's shed. Kerosene lanterns dangled from nails driven into the overhead beams. All across one whole section of wall were rows and rows of horseshoes hooked on rods. Near them was a giant anvil. People like Marty called the farrier to do all that horseshoe work. I guess that was just another thing the Rhinestats did on their own.

Mr. Rhinestat told me to go ahead and turn out Rainy Day so he could have some fun with the buggy horses out in the pasture. I did, and he galloped out to join them.

After we had finished moving the hay, I found myself sitting with the whole family at a long wooden dining table. Ammann turned out to be friendly and not at all weird or reserved with me as I had been afraid he would be. Sometimes when boys your own age meet you with their parents around, they behave strangely. Ammann seemed perfectly natural. Esther was on one side of me and Rachel, her younger sister, was on the other. The other kids—Luther and Will—sat across from me. Baby Dirk sat in a high chair. Before we ate, everyone bowed their heads and said a quiet blessing for food and family. And then Mrs. Rhinestat, Esther, and even little Rachel rose and brought out the meal. For lunchtime in the middle of August it seemed like huge amount of food: pot roast, boiled potatoes, braised carrots glazed in brown sugar, pickled beets, fresh bread, and butter. Everyone, including the adults, drank milk. For dessert we had strawberry-rhubarb pie.

Over lunch I told Mr. Rhinestat about how Aunt Patti had been hired to do the flowers for Barbara Follette's daughter's wedding.

"She's the commissioner behind the buggy tax," I said. "And the cell phone tower thing. I know that she's planning to push it all the way through to the federal courts if necessary."

Mrs. Rhinestat looked at her husband but didn't say anything.

Mr. Rhinestat drank the last of his milk and put down his glass. "Yes, it came up again at a meeting of our elders," he said. "All of us are getting letters in the mail about this matter. It is a problem that will not go away on its own. It would be very much against our custom to accommodate one of those towers on land where not even car engines belong. We do not scorn the ways of the world, but we choose to live apart from them. For some English this is difficult to accept."

It *was* difficult for me to accept some of their choices, but I didn't say anything.

"We do not understand why Mrs. Follette has decided to push us into a corner on these matters. I suppose our wheels do gouge the gravel roads, but I do not understand the necessity of placing the tower on our property."

"I guess people like her think it's better if cell phone connections didn't cut off in the more rural parts of the state," I said.

Nelson had been complaining since he arrived about this very subject. I knew Aunt Patti would have felt more comfortable with me going on longer rides alone if she could reach me on a cell phone, but even as I said it, it seemed ridiculous. What regular people thought was convenient and good, the Amish thought was unnecessary and threatening to their way of life. These people didn't even have normal telephones, let alone cell phones. How could they begin to understand why the rest of the world wanted to be able to make a phone call no matter where on the planet they happened to be? The family just sat there looking at me.

"Part of it must be this woman," I said. "My aunt is going crazy working for her. She keeps changing her mind about everything. And the wedding is really soon."

Mr. Rhinestat shrugged, and I realized that there was no way he could understand how a modern wedding could be stressful on a florist or why it had to be. In his world, food and flowers were provided by the community.

"So, JP is doing great," I said, changing the subject.

"He's training on the lead rope now." I explained how cute he had been, and what a good colt we all thought he would be one day.

"You are good with horses, April," Mr. Rhinestat said as I fell in with the customs of the house and rose to clear the dishes with Esther, Rachel, and Mrs. Rhinestat. "I could tell that from the moment you showed up on our drive."

In spite of feeling drawn into a serving role, I felt I had received one of the best compliments ever. If this family considered me a natural with horses, I could begin to think of myself that way, too. So what if the men and boys got to sit while the girls and women cleared the dishes? That was the way life worked in that house. I would save gender equity for home, where—at least at our house—females ruled.

The next day I was at Room for Blooms trying not to do anything that made Aunt Patti more exasperated than she was already. It was Wednesday, and the Follette wedding was only three days away. And the original centerpiece Aunt Patti had designed for the dinner following the ceremony had been unexpectedly vetoed by Mrs. Follette.

Aunt Patti had proposed carving watermelon halves into pretty shapes, and then filling them with all kinds of fruit, flowers, and greens that would spill out from the center of each one. If they wanted to, guests could have nibbled on the grapes and cherries that would have been like a giant fruit basket. A tall hyacinth would have been placed at the center of each arrangement. Aunt Patti thought these would have been perfect for a late summer reception. She had ordered all the fruit, and now thirty watermelons and cases of fruit were piled up in the back room of the shop.

All was well until the night before, when Mrs. Follette called up. She didn't even say hello before she started talking.

"On second thought, I want something more classic. I suggest glass vases filled with white and yellow roses, and lots of baby's breath and greens around the edges."

"I'll give her baby's breath around the edges," Aunt Patti muttered as I helped her clear the fruit out of the working area. "I've already paid for all this fruit. Now, just to cover my costs, I'm going to have to charge something wild for the change. I hope I can lay my hands on enough roses at the last minute."

Picking up a heavy watermelon and carrying it to the growing pile in the back, I wanted to say that at least we wouldn't have to worry about eating enough fruit for the rest of the summer, but didn't think Aunt Patti would appreciate the comment. She was placing a crate of dark red cherries in the walk-in refrigerator.

"I'm going to have to hire extra help, *extra* extra help," she said. "And of course now I've got to get my hands on thirty vases. We may need to drive into St. Louis this afternoon. Assuming I can get them, I'll need all of Thursday and Friday to make the arrangements. Once I've got the roses, I'll need to get into the venue and set everything up on Saturday. All of this, apart from the large arrangements we've planned for the church itself, not to mention the bride's bouquet, the bridesmaids' bouquets, the flower girl's basket, and the boutonnieres for the groomsmen and the fathers of the bride and groom."

Aunt Patti threw herself against the back door and heaved something between a sigh and a moan. "April, tell me everything is going to come out all right," she said.

"Everything is going to come out all right."

She laughed. "Oh, thank you, now I feel fine."

I took our candy dish from the counter and held it out to her. "Sometimes all a person can do is eat gumdrops," I said.

"You're right about that," Aunt Patti said, reaching into the bowl.

This was the private joke we made whenever life got overwhelming. It was usually me who felt anxious—mostly with homework or social pressure. Sometimes I suffered one of my "orphaned-at-four pangs" and needed some kind of small boost. The saying "sometimes all you can do is," which Aunt Patti and I completed with things like "watch a dumb movie," "go out for ice cream," "take a warm bath," or "eat brownies," helped us get through some tough situations. It wasn't a cure—usually Aunt Patti made me talk things out, too—but it always helped.

"You want me to drive into St. Louis with you for this stuff?" I asked after we had each munched through a handful of gumdrops.

"I need to think about the logistics here, but thank you for the offer. Or maybe Fran will be free. First I need to make some calls and see what's available supply-wise." Aunt Patti paused, considering her words carefully. "The thing is, I need to do this reception right, because the Follettes are very socially connected around here, and one job will lead to another."

"I get it."

The little string of bells attached to the front door of the shop jingled, and we looked up to see Nelson walk in with a big smile on his face.

"Hey there," he said.

"Hey, Nelson," Aunt Patti said. "What brings you into the big city?"

"Just farm-related stuff, no big deal. Pop slacked off a little with the red tape in the last year. I've been over at the county offices straightening things out. I had to go through piles of claims and statements and, from what I could see, Plattsburgh had to do some serious public works upgrading in May. I mean, I knew things got hairy here, but I had no idea how dreadful things were. Drains had to be reconfigured and sewer lines updated. You guys must have had a lot of water damage."

"No kidding," Aunt Patti said. "Just ask April here if

you want the details. We lost at least a dozen trailer homes, and whole neighborhoods flooded. It was a miracle nobody died, actually. April saw to that."

Skipping most of the details, I explained to Nelson the whole story of how Rainy Day and I managed to rescue Shawn Clarke, the wheelchair-bound young veteran who was trapped in his trailer home as the water rose.

"Jeez," Nelson said to me when I was done. "And here I thought you were merely a mild-mannered farmhand."

I shrugged.

"So how's the wedding coming?" he asked Aunt Patti.

"It's coming," she said. "And that's about all I can say right now."

"Mrs. Follette just changed her mind about the centerpieces," I said.

"What? Three days before the event?" Nelson's pale face flushed pink out of sympathy with Aunt Patti.

"What can I do?" Aunt Patti said. "I'm over it. Now I just have to make sure she gets what she wants."

"People like her usually do," Nelson said. "While I was over at the county offices, I couldn't help but poke into that situation with the Amish she's got going. Remember the story that April showed us last week? It's really quite unbelievable. There's that special fee the town wants to collect for the buggies, which on the surface seems fair but in context it's not at all right. Those people pay all kinds of taxes for services they don't use. I don't see why this community can't share the burden of road maintenance. It's not like those wheels are wreaking havoc on the environment."

"I think she wants to force them away," I said. "I mean, think about it...she wants to make them so miserable and unwelcome that they just decide to pick up and settle in some other town."

I had picked up a daisy off the floor and was twirling it in my hand. Aunt Patti and Nelson stared at me. Everything I had heard and seen for the last few months was beginning to add up.

"I think that's what Mr. Rhinestat thinks, too," I continued. "They don't talk about it, but that's how people like him think. They see it as just like what happened to their people in Europe four hundred years ago. Same thing with the cell phone tower deal. The outside world, the English, are trying to force them to change because of the way they live."

"Remind me of the cell phone thing?" Aunt Patti asked.

"They're pressuring Mr. Rhinestat to put a tower up on his land," I said. "And people like Mrs. Follette can't understand why he won't make the deal."

"Yeah, I looked into that, too," Nelson said. "Seems that our friend Barbara Follette has a little bit of interest in BeneTran's presence here in Plattsburgh. She owns stock in the company, and if they get their tower, they'll be able to charge more because their service will be better. They charge more for service, they earn more profit. They earn more profit, and guess who makes more money? The shareholders. Suddenly it's not just about bringing Plattsburgh into the twenty-first century. It's about more money for herself."

At home that afternoon, I lay on my bed and listened to music on my portable music player. As I patted Chase, who was lying on the end of my bed, I looked around my room and thought about what I would have to get rid of if I were an Amish girl. The music player, of course, and the clock radio that woke me up every morning. My earrings and other jewelry. I'd have to switch all my clothes for plain long dresses and get rid of most of my shoes. In the bathroom, there was my blow dryer. And Aunt Patti and I shared a set of hot rollers and a straightener. All of these things would go. Usually I didn't wear makeup, but I did have mascara, blush, and half a dozen tubes of lip-glosses. There were one or two bottles of polish I sometimes put on my toenails. Oh, yes, and in the back of my closet, all jumbled on the floor, were a few old toys I used to play with that took batteries. I would have to pitch them, too.

What would be left? I wondered. I closed my eyes. And as I lay there listening to one of my favorite top-ten songs, the one all my friends thought was the best, I realized that the real question was: *Who* would be left? Without all my stuff, what kind of person would I be?

chapter

I woke up from a nap just in time to ride over to the McCann place for evening chores. It was nearly five o'clock when I arrived and turned out Rainy Day to join Hannah and JP in the paddock. The day was dry, hot, and sunny. All the chickens were gathered in the shade under the pickup truck, listlessly pecking at nothing much. In his pen, old Moses stood in the dirt twitching his tail. One of the white geese honked as I approached the barn, then turned away as if even that was too much bother. I went straight to the barn and started mucking out the stalls and seeing that all the rest of the animals had the food and water they needed. I climbed up into the hayloft to check on the supplies of grain and hay. Even just twelve feet off the ground, the air grew hotter and more still. A swallow dove down past me as I crawled through the opening in the floorboards.

Not everything was quiet. Apart from the buzz of insects, I could hear the ring of constant and steady hammer blows. Two hammers at work, banging at two different pitches. It must have been Lowell and Nelson replacing the roof of the storage shed. As far as I knew, they had been at it since the morning. The shed wasn't big, but there was a lot of wood to get on there, and with just the two of them it had turned into a big job. I went over to the shed to see their progress.

Both Nelson and Lowell were squatting on the roof, hammering away. Nails were clamped in their teeth and they both were concentrating so hard that they didn't notice me standing there. A stack of planks leaned up against the side of the shed and a big cardboard box of asphalt shingles was beside it.

"Hey, Lowell!" I shouted above the hammering.

"Oh, hey, April."

Nelson looked over his shoulder and smiled down at me. They were both beet red in the face and sweaty.

"You guys want a drink or anything?"

"Some water'd be great," Nelson said. "Thanks."

Since Mr. McCann had died, Nelson and Lowell had completely repaired all the messed-up porch steps and replaced the broken or loose balusters in the rickety porch rail. You could still tell the old from the new wood, but eventually Nelson would paint the whole thing and you would never even know the difference. Climbing up past the rocker where Mr. McCann always sat in those last weeks, I suddenly felt like maybe I ought to have paid closer attention to him. He would have been so happy to see the place cared for and to have his son home. It was a shame he would never get to see things fixed up.

Even the kitchen wasn't the dump it had been when he would send me in to fetch his butter cake and cold coffee. Everything was clean, and the refrigerator was stocked with fresh milk, fruit, and real live vegetables, not frozen blocks of spinach. It was easy to find two glasses and a pitcher. The ice tray was filled with cubes.

I took the glasses and pitcher out to the shed, set them on the cement stoop, and called up to Nelson and Lowell that water was there whenever they were ready. Without missing a single beat in the hammering, they said thanks in unison.

On my way to the paddock I stopped by the barn and got JP's lead line and halter. In my pocket I had a handful of alfalfa cubes for rewards and encouragement.

As soon as JP saw me standing on the rail of the fence, he came trotting over. Thanks to Marty's good advice, I always offered something to JP—treats, praise, pats, scratches—that made him associate only good things with me. When he saw me, he didn't think *work*, he thought *happiness*.

"Good boy," I said, greeting him with rubs all over his face and around his ears. I offered him an alfalfa cube out of my hand, and he nibbled it up with his soft, flexible lips. Then I put on his halter and clipped on the lead rope. After just a few training sessions I had been able to get rid of the part that looped around his hindquarters, and now we were working on turns, backing up, and moving through narrow openings. In the next few days, I knew Marty wanted to see if we could get him to follow Hannah into a horse trailer, but for now I was supposed to just get him comfortable walking in and out of gate openings.

"First period begins now, JP," I said quietly.

Like kindergarten parents watching from the outside of a school yard, Hannah and Rainy Day stood together under a tree and kept an eye on JP's progress. Hannah pretended to graze, but I could tell she knew exactly what JP was up to at all times. She was another reason I never wanted JP to protest what I wanted. If he seemed stressed, or shoved me off balance, he'd call out for her and she would come over. And chances are she would come over angry.

JP did great. Half an hour later, I removed the halter and lead line and headed toward the paddock gate. I always liked to let him play freely for a while before putting the halter back on and leading him into the barn.

Turning to the gate, I was surprised to see Lowell and Nelson hanging on the rail, talking quietly.

"How long have you guys been here?" I asked, hooking the bent wire loop on to the peg to fix the gate shut.

"Not long," Lowell said.

"It's weird how you get so focused on training you don't even notice anything going on around you," I said.

"Thirsty?" Nelson offered me a cold can of soda.

"Where'd you find that?"

"Basement fridge," he said. "Just one of the many secret wonders of this house. A few days ago I remembered that my mom always kept a second fridge. It was standing behind ten folding chairs, a broken ping-pong table, and my sister's play kitchen. Anyway, Lowell cleaned it out, brave soul that he is, and I just stocked it yesterday."

"Thanks," I said, grateful for the soda.

It was getting close to seven o'clock, time to get JP and Hannah back in the barn, then saddle up Rainy Day and leave well before the sun went down. Lowell's mom pulled up to take him home, and Nelson kept me company while I finished the chores.

"You know, April," he said, "I've been thinking all day about this, and I think that while I'm here in town I might as well offer my services to the Rhinestats."

"What do you mean, your services?" I asked.

"I mean, legal counsel. My professional services, as we say."

I was tightening the girth. Rainy Day liked a nice snug saddle.

"Thinking about what those folks are up against, it's just not right that they ought to be singled out by one powerful person acting out of self-interest," Nelson explained.

"Maybe she thinks her best interest is also the town's best interest," I said.

Nelson snorted but said nothing. The subject had been worrying me, too, but from another angle.

"I just wonder about people who choose not to participate in basic modern life. I know Barbara Follette is not a nice person and all, but isn't it . . . I don't know . . . rude, to reject the way the rest of the world is living?"

"We can approve or not approve of their choices about how they live their lives, April," Nelson said. "But I'm talking about the law. And our laws do not allow the government to push individual people around. People have certain rights and freedoms, and you are not entitled to put them at a disadvantage just because you don't care for their personal choices."

Nelson yanked a long dry dandelion from the ground and waved it around until the white seeds drifted into the wind.

"One of the things I've learned from reading all these old newspaper clippings piled up around here is that Pop was a big believer in local government doing right by the community it represents. The Rhinestats can say no to my offer, but I would like to make myself available to them. I *am* a public defender, after all. They're just a different demographic than I'm used to dealing with."

He let the bare dandelion stem fall to the ground.

That night I told Aunt Patti what Nelson had decided to do. She took off her glasses and rubbed her eyes. Her wild hair was tousled around her face and the tips of her fingers were stained green from handling stems all day. I rotated my corn on the cob in the stick of butter, salted it carefully all around, and chomped into the first delicious sweet bite. Fresh corn was one of the best things about August.

"I wonder what he's thinking," she said, pursing her lips.

"I think he thinks it's just not fair."

"Yeah, well, thinking something's not fair is not the same thing as doing something about it. I hope he waits until after the wedding."

"But Mrs. Follette doesn't know you and he are friends or anything, right?"

"No…"

"Or more than friends?" I couldn't help but add.

Aunt Patti grinned into her corn but otherwise ignored my comment. "Follette will be a happier mother-of-the-bride if nobody's getting her all riled up. And a happier mother-of-the-bride means a more patient client for me."

"Hmm, I see your point. The thing is, Nelson doesn't even know if the Rhinestats will want him to represent them. He's just going to make the offer."

"I guess that's some consolation," she said, picking up her corn. "And I guess it also makes me wonder what's going on with him and his real work in St. Louis. You haven't heard him mention his future intentions, have you?"

She eyeballed me intently over the top of her corn. I pretended not to notice that for her own personal reasons she was digging for insider information.

"I know he doesn't want to leave until the farm is ready for resale," I said casually, but I had the very strong suspicion that Aunt Patti was more than a little bit interested in what Nelson McCann decided to do. It was the one thing she didn't seem to be able to ask him directly.

The next morning I bumped into Aunt Patti making coffee in the kitchen at the crack of dawn.

"How come you're up?" I said, pouring my usual cold cereal mixture—a third of each of my favorite brands.

She explained that she was on her way into St. Louis to get to the various suppliers first thing. The wholesale flower market opened at eight o'clock, and all the rest at nine. If all went well, she could be back with plenty of afternoon to prep for the wedding.

"That gives me this afternoon and all day Friday," she said. "Saturday we can get into the hall and the church and do what needs to be done. I've asked Fran and a few other people to come in part-time in the next couple of days to see me through this." She sighed. "When this is all over I think I'll buy a one-way ticket to Fiji."

She picked up her purse and headed for the back door. "Have a good day, April," she called over her shoulder, pulling the door shut behind her.

It was nice having the whole house to myself so early. I

didn't have to tiptoe around, worrying about waking Aunt Patti or shushing Chase, who usually barked to be let out, where he could bark even more at the rabbits grazing on the lawn. I put my bowl and spoon in the dishwasher and got on with my routine. I brushed my teeth, knotted my hair into a bun, grabbed my backpack from the peg by the door, and went out to the barn.

Rainy Day must have heard Aunt Patti leave, because he was wide-awake in his stall. As soon as I walked in, he turned and nickered at me. I patted him on the hind-quarters and swept my hand around to his front until I got to his head. I swung open the window to let him see out. Then I gave him a scoop of oats to munch on while I saddled him for the day. Before leaving, I locked Chase back in the house. "See you later, boy."

We arrived at the McCann place at the usual time. After turning out Rainy Day, I was surprised to find Nelson in the henhouse, gathering eggs. Normally, that was one of the things I did every day.

"Hey there, April," he said. "I woke up at three and couldn't fall back to sleep. I read for a while, but when it got to be five-thirty I thought I may as well come out and make myself useful."

Nelson had dark hollows under his eyes but seemed

fine otherwise. I went about my business as usual. JP whinnied at me from his stall.

"I'll be with you in a little bit," I said. "I know you want to get out and play. Just hang on."

But JP wouldn't just hang on. He didn't stop kicking at his wall and whinnying. All his racket got the other animals all riled up, including Hannah, and I realized that I would have to rethink my routine.

"Oh, all right," I said, approaching their stall. "Let's get you guys outside. If you want to do some training this early, it's fine with me, I guess."

I could barely get JP to settle down enough to put on his halter. He was so excited and jumpy, I had to use my sharpest tone to get his head under control. With the six-foot lead, we went out to the corral for the morning lesson.

Immediately I could tell things were not going to go smoothly. JP fought even the simplest moves. It was like he had forgotten everything he had learned. He pulled, resisted, bucked, and reared. He seemed to want to do the opposite of everything I wanted him to do. I was losing my patience and it began to show. I yanked on the lead to follow, spoke in a sharp tone of voice, and stamped my foot.

"No, JP. What do you think you're doing? I said we're

going this way and I mean it. We're going *this* way."

I leaned with all my weight into his shoulder until I felt him start the turn.

There must have been something in that shove, or maybe in my tone, because as soon as JP made the turn, he suddenly stopped resisting and looked me right in the eye. It was as if he was saying, *Oh, I get it, you really aren't going to let me get away with this, are you?* I looked him square in the eye, took a deep breath, and said, "No, I am not. You have to do what I say and that's that." I had learned enough from Marty to know that a horse could only be happy if he felt secure following the will of a strong leader.

From then on it was like we were back where we had been. I had a nice obedient foal again. Over and over again for the next twenty minutes we made figure eights, and backed up, and passed through the gate. All this time when he cooperated, I patted him and gave him treats.

Soon he was turned out with Hannah, happily suckling in the long grass. Rainy Day was standing nearby, grazing and swishing his tail swiftly to the left, then swiftly to the right in rhythmic swipes. Standing on the pasture fence looking in, I realized that JP must have been testing me. He had to learn for himself that when a human was around, he would really have no choice about what to do.

Before leaving for the middle of the day, I collapsed on the porch just to sit. Nelson joined me with two glasses of juice.

"Are you free for a little while, April?"

"Sort of. I guess. I'm pretty tired, though. Why?"

"I'm hoping you'll stick with me a little bit today. You know the Rhinestats. I was thinking of driving over there to make my offer. Assuming they accept, I'll need to head over to town hall to try to identify a precedent in the records that will help establish my case. Their two cases. I'm sure they'd feel more comfortable if you were with me."

I agreed to go, and we left around eleven o'clock. Mr. Rhinestat was in the barn with Ammann, mending tack. They were repairing loose buckles and tightening harness straps. I introduced Nelson to them.

"Glad to meet you, Mr. McCann," Mr. Rhinestat said. "I was sorry to hear about your father's passing."

"Thank you. Yeah, it was pretty sudden. Now I'm just trying to get the place fixed up. With April here's help, of course. We're actually here today because I heard about your situation with the local leaders."

"It's difficult for us," Mr. Rhinestat said. "We try to live and let live."

"I know you do," Nelson said. "That's why I'd like to

try to offer my services, if you'll allow me to. I'm an attorney and would be happy to take this on pro bono."

"Pro bono?" I asked. "What's that mean?"

Nelson chuckled. "That means for free."

Mr. Rhinestat considered the offer gravely. I was sure he would say no thanks, so I was surprised and relieved when he reached out to clasp Nelson's hand.

"You may be the answer to our prayers," he said gratefully. "We do not want to make trouble for anyone, and we will do what we have to do to be law abiding. Our community would be obliged to you if you could help us accomplish that much, while also concluding this in a way that's fair to everyone."

Mr. Rhinestat took off his straw hat and wiped his forehead and the back of his neck with a hanky. He had farm work to do, and I could tell he was relieved that he could go about his business with one less "outside world" thing to think about.

The inside of the county office building was nice and cool. We climbed up the wide front steps and entered a spacious rotunda. We made no sound walking across the waxed wooden floor. The walls around us were marble, and there were carved sculptures of various Greek gods near the ceiling. High above a doorway at the east end of the spacious entrance, foot-high letters spelled justice. At the west end, over another wide doorway, the carved letters spelled mercy. Around the border of the hall were six-foot-tall columns with busts of American presidents on top—carved into each column were quotations by that president.

Nelson took a deep breath and consulted a directory behind glass to determine where we needed to go first. The offices were upstairs above the rotunda. We could get to them either by a wide stairway that curved around the outside of the main hall or by an elevator. Records were downstairs in a bunker-like chamber. Since Plattsburgh was built in a watershed—smack in the middle of rivers and streams—everything belowground had to be protected against flood.

"First things first," he said. "I need to have a look through the complete Plattsburgh tax code. We'll go to the archives for that."

We took the elevator to the second floor and approached a big wooden desk where a woman sat typing information into a computer. She looked up.

"May I help y'all?"

"Please," Nelson said. "We're looking for the tax code volumes."

The woman led us to a library stack, gestured to the shelves with a smile, and returned to her work.

Nelson pulled out a dark maroon hardbound book and took it over to a Ping-Pong-size table. He pulled out a yellow legal pad from his satchel, opened the heavy oversize book, and started scribbling notes on the top sheet of paper.

While he was writing, I noticed a woman come out of the elevator and step briskly to the secretary's desk.

"I need the land-use records, Sue," the woman said. "Also the eminent domain regulations."

I had no idea what she was asking for but the secretary hopped to it.

"No problem, Mrs. Follette. It'll just be a sec."

Barbara Follette! Nelson was so busy studying the tax codes that he didn't hear the name. I elbowed him and took the pen out of his hand. On the legal pad I wrote:

That woman is Barbara Follette. Go talk to her!

Nelson widened his eyes and got up from the table. He walked over to Mrs. Follette, who was half-sitting on the secretary's table, facing away from us. She had short dark hair cut into a helmet-like shape. She wore a cream-colored pants suit and coral beads around her throat. While she waited, she seemed to be examining her fingernails.

"Mrs. Follette?"

"Yes?"

"My name is Nelson McCann. Joseph McCann was my father," he said, extending his right hand.

"Yes, of course. I was sorry to hear about Joe. He rather disappeared from sight after your mother passed." She shook his hand in return.

"Yes, thank you. He did go somewhat underground, I know. Well, it's funny I should run into you. I was just looking into this matter of the buggy tax—"

"Oh, don't get me started," she said, interrupting. "Those people are the bane of my existence these days."

"Yes, well, I am—"

Nelson was obviously trying to convey the fact that he was representing "those people," but Mrs. Follette would not let him finish his thought.

"Why they think they can just set themselves up wherever they want and simply flaunt their non-conformity is beyond me. Not to mention hold the rest of the town hostage to their customs."

"Are you referring to John Rhinestat refusing to accommodate the cell phone tower?" Nelson asked.

"Of course I am. If companies like BeneTran think of us as a backwater, we will remain a backwater. It's as simple as that. The county is at its wit's end over this thing. We want and need to see development and growth here in Plattsburgh. And right now we're stuck. I had been hoping to have this all resolved before my daughter's wedding this weekend, but it looks like that will be out of the question."

Nelson didn't mention anything about knowing Aunt Patti, or that he knew about the wedding.

The secretary came back with an armful of oversize books that she passed to Mrs. Follette. "Do you need a hand getting these back to your office, Mrs. Follette?"

"I think I can manage, Sylvia. Thank you." She peered at Nelson over the tops of the giant volumes. "Please give my condolences to your whole family."

"I sure will," Nelson said. He returned to our table.

"You didn't mention that you were taking up their case," I said as Nelson went back to studying the tax codes.

"Nope, I didn't," he said. "You never show your hand before the time is right, April," he said, cuffing me under the chin. "And the time was definitely not right. We'll have a lot more leeway in settling this thing if we do our homework in private."

I crossed my arms on the table and put my head down.

The one thing that stuck with me was Mrs. Follette's saying "those people." I was pretty sure I had once done that, too—called them "those people." I had never given the words much thought before now, but hearing them from Mrs. Follette made me feel bad. What was it about people that made us call anyone different from us "those people"?

Friday came and went in a blur. I didn't see Nelson at all. He was probably back at town hall trying to dig up anything that might make a better case for the Rhinestats. Aunt Patti practically moved into Room for Blooms on Thursday afternoon after returning from St. Louis. She came home to sleep long after I went to bed, and was up and gone early the next morning before I woke up. The only signs that she had come home were her wet toothbrush in the bathroom and the soggy coffee filter in the kitchen trash. For the past thirty-six hours, we had basically kept in touch by phone.

On Saturday morning I came home after chores and took a shower. Aunt Patti was waiting for us. She had recruited Lowell and me to help transfer all the arrangements to the church and banquet hall for the wedding setup. Lowell and I piled into the pickup and went over to Room for Blooms, where Miz Fran met us.

"Be careful," Aunt Patti warned as we began hauling the heavy vases and arrangements into the back of the truck. "Don't trip."

"I've never seen so many roses before in my life," Miz Fran said, her face hidden behind a row of vases all jammed into the bottom of a cardboard box so they wouldn't slide around.

"Jeez, I know," Lowell said, crouching forward in the truck bed to receive the box.

"It's nearly eleven, which means we don't have time to make more than one trip," Aunt Patti said, coming out from the shop carrying a plastic tarp. "What doesn't fit in the truck we've got to get into your car, Fran. Here, April," she said, tossing the tarp into my arms. "Spread this out across her backseat."

Our first stop was the First United Methodist Church of Plattsburgh. Each holding on to an iron handle, Aunt Patti and Lowell carried in the first of several enormous urns that were going to sit by the pulpit and elsewhere around the sanctuary. Tall blades of spiky green leaves formed the background of the arrangements, while a mixture of big round balls of white chrysanthemums and purple flowers stood in front. Some kind of pretty vine draped up and over the front rim of the urns and dangled to the red carpet on the floor. I followed behind, carrying the box with the bride's bouquet, the flower girl's basket, the bridesmaids' bouquets, and the groomsmen's boutonnieres. Everything was sitting in little tubes of water clamped into place and surrounded by freezer packs.

Once they had placed the urn into position, I watched Aunt Patti rotate it until she was satisfied with how it would look to the congregation. She wiped her hands on her jeans and pushed up her glasses.

"Move on, troops."

Lowell saluted and spun around on his heel. He and I marched back up the aisle like soldiers. When the rest of the urns were in place, we got back in the truck and drove to our next stop, Marie's Vineyard and Winery, about eight miles out of town. On our way we passed the McCann farm.

"Hey," I said as we got to the very same fork where Boone's Passage splits off from Cedar Falls Road, "down that way is the Rhinestat place. I never realized how close to the river they were."

By noon we were slowly winding up a long driveway toward a solitary house on a rise. I had to admit it was a beautiful location for a party. Right on a woodsy bend of the river, all set back on a long lawn, it was a big old-fashioned two-story white house. We pulled up to the service entrance and saw the caterer's van and a few other cars parked by the kitchen door. Farther toward the rear of the house was a screened-in wraparound porch that looked out on the river.

"Sweet!" Lowell said, having gotten out first.

"This is very nice," his mom said. "Patti, this is going to look so lovely."

"I sure hope so," she said. "But I'll only be able to relax when it's over. Let me go in and make sure the tables are ready for us, linens are on, and all that. Hang on just a sec."

Lowell and I walked over to look at the view from the river side of the building. At the bottom of the long sloping lawn, the water sparkled in the hot sun and rippled into tiny waves by the breeze. There was a path leading from the back of the house to the water's edge. A little dock stuck out into the water, and a small outboard rowboat bobbed against the wood.

"I'd love to go down and swim," he said.

"I know, I'm boiling," I agreed.

Aunt Patti called us back up to the service entrance.

"April, Lowell, let's get unloaded. Cross your fingers that nothing tipped over back here."

As soon as we put one foot inside the house, Lowell and I exchanged looks. It was a crazy scene, and the stress level of every single person we saw was over the top. The caterer was running around with a clipboard, yelling at waiters and taking inventory. The winery/hotel manager was trailing after him, trying to get his attention. The photographer was setting up the picture-taking corner. A videographer was sorting through cables and equipment. Maintenance people were nailing the final pieces of a dance floor into place. And to top it off, a five-piece band was setting up all their instruments and amplifiers on a wooden riser at one end of the large dining room.

"Remind me to elope," Lowell muttered.

"You and me both," I said. Lowell looked at me and raised his eyebrows. I laughed.

"I don't mean together," I said. "Just, I agree. Hey, look over on the porch. In that straw chair with the big back. It's a kid."

It looked like Aunt Patti wasn't quite ready for us yet, so we went over to the kid in the chair. He was crouched over his lap, playing a video game. He was concentrating so hard, he didn't notice us approach.

"Hi!" I said.

The kid looked up. "Hi!"

"Are you in the band?" Lowell joked.

"Ha-ha," the boy said, waggling his thumbs on his gaming thing.

"So what are you doing here?" I asked.

166

"It's my sister's stupid wedding today and my mom made me come with her because everyone was too busy to stay with me and she didn't want to leave me at home alone because the house is perfectly clean."

"Your sister's wedding?" I said. "So your mom is Mrs. Follette?"

"Mmmm."

"She's here now?"

"Mmmm."

This news made me a little nervous. I didn't think Mrs. Follette would remember me from the other day at town hall, but I wasn't sure. With a daughter getting married, I was surprised she had a kid this young.

"What's your name?" I asked the boy.

"Brandon."

"I'm April. And this is Lowell."

Lowell sat down on the floor next to Brandon. "Dude, it's not so bad here."

Brandon stopped thumbing at his game and looked up. "It is so. All the guys in my class went to Six Flags today and I couldn't go. Then they're all having a sleepover at this kid Jeremy's house. And I can't do that, either, because I have to be here."

Lowell shrugged.

Just then we heard Aunt Patti call us back into the main dining room. "Kids, let's go. We can start bringing things in."

"See you," I said to Brandon.

We were suddenly part of the mass mayhem in the dining room. I tried not to bump into anyone as I made repeated trips from the truck, carrying glass vases filled with gorgeous roses in bloom. I had just lowered my third vase when behind me I heard the voice I had heard in town hall.

"And I am telling *you* that I want that cake here no later than three-thirty. You are just going to have to make some sort of arrangement so that will happen. Any later is quite frankly unacceptable to me."

I turned and saw the caterer groveling before Mrs. Follette.

"I know exactly how you feel," he said. "And I've spoken with the baker. It's a custom job, as you know, and he wants every last detail to be just perfect. He's afraid he won't be able to rely on the temperature in the kitchen here this afternoon, that's all. He assures me it's for the best."

"But there could be traffic. There could be some other delay. I just—"

"Mom!"

Brandon had approached his mom from behind in full whine-mode. I braced myself for the worst.

She wheeled around and practically hissed. "Brandon, I have asked you repeatedly to sit patiently for just a few minutes."

"But Mom, I'm so bored. And I'm hungry. Did you bring anything for lunch?"

Mrs. Follette's exasperation filled the whole dining room. "Brandon Pierre Follette. This is your sister's wedding day. There's a lot going on. I realize you're just hanging around but that's what we need you to do. And I have to say that I think a boy of eight should be perfectly capable of entertaining himself for one or two hours on the most special day of his sister's life. Please. Just go sit down. It'll just be a few more minutes."

She turned back to the caterer, who was probably relieved that she took at least a little bit of her frustration out on her kid. Everything Mrs. Follette had said seemed perfectly calculated to drive any normal kid crazy, and before I turned to go back to the truck for another vase, I saw Brandon's face flush red and his eyes fill with tears.

Wedged in the narrow space behind the seat of the pickup I found a package of candy and an old comic book. On my next trip in, I stopped by the porch and offered them to Brandon, who was back in his chair thumbing furiously at his video game. I never saw anyone's face go from bunched and angry to grateful in so short a time.

"Thanks," he said.

Driving back home, Lowell said he thought Brandon was a real brat. "What kind of kid can't realize that Six Flags and a sleepover come second to a sister's wedding?" he said. "Something's screwed up there."

"Yeah, well, he was pretty mad. And his mom was giving him a hard time," I said. "She's hard on everyone, and her son is no exception."

In spite of what I had just said, a part of me agreed with Lowell about Brandon. Still, a bigger part of me—the foal trainer part of me—was thinking that Brandon was just getting a bad education.

chapter

We got home around three o'clock, and I was relieved to be done with my role in the wedding business.

"You want to stay and watch a movie?" I asked Lowell, who looked as exhausted as I felt.

"Sure," he said.

Aunt Patti had just enough time to shower, dress, and get back to the church to set up the wedding party with their various flowers. Just as I flopped onto the couch, the phone rang.

"April, can you get that, babe?" Aunt Patti called from her room. "I'm on the fly but it could be Mrs. Follette."

I picked up. "Hello?"

"This is Tony Stewart, from Marie's Vineyard and Winery. I'm trying to reach Patti Helmbach. There's no answer at Room for Blooms."

"She can't come to the phone right now. Can I take a message?"

I was distracted from the caller because Lowell had flipped channels to cage fighting, and cage fighting was out of the question for the afternoon entertainment. I waggled my finger to signal an emphatic no.

"I'm sorry," the voice on the phone insisted. "But it's a bit of an emergency. Is there any way I can reach her right now?"

I stopped goofing around and paid attention. "Hang on."

I put the phone down and ran into the bathroom. Aunt Patti was just stepping into the shower. "Who is it?"

"It's the manager from the reception place. He says it's an emergency."

Aunt Patti swore under her breath, threw on her bathrobe, and took the phone into the kitchen. I put the TV on mute and told Lowell what was going on. When Aunt Patti came back in a few minutes later, her hand holding the phone was dangly limply at her side.

"You look pretty grim," I said. "What's up?"

"Some little kid, Mrs. Follette's son, is missing. I don't remember seeing a child there but they can't find him. He's been missing for almost an hour. Follette's been questioning everybody, going crazy, as you can imagine. One of the waiters told this Tony that they had last noticed a boy talking to you, April. So they're wondering if we know anything. *Do* you know anything?"

I was speechless. Lowell jumped right in. "Well, we know that he was miserable, and that his mom yelled at him and made him feel bad about being miserable."

"She didn't exactly yell," I said.

"You know what I mean."

"He probably just took off," I said. "There's a nice path down to the river. A dock and everything. He probably just got sick of sitting on that porch waiting around."

"The river?" Aunt Patti looked horrified.

"I doubt he went down to the river," Lowell said. "I bet he went into the woods where it was shady. April gave him a book, right? And some candy?"

I nodded.

"In any case, Mrs. Follette has contacted the sheriff's office," Aunt Patti said. "Tony said to call him back if we can help at all. Obviously, everything's on hold until Mrs. Follette's son is found. But I should probably finish getting ready and go over to the reception place to help look for him."

I wasn't sure what to do. I didn't feel right sitting there and watching television, but what could I do to help?

"Hey, Lowell, tell Aunt Patti I'll see her later. And I'll catch up with you over at McCann's. I'm going to take Rainy Day out. Maybe we can help search."

Rainy Day blinked a few times when he saw me appear in the barn in the middle of the afternoon with his bridle in my hand.

"I know you're used to a little longer siesta, Rainy Day, but this is an exception," I said, patting his sides, scratching his ears, and watching him mouth at the bit to settle it in place.

I led him out of his stall and to the end of the driveway, then mounted into the saddle and clucked him forward.

I didn't have a plan, but figured we should head off in the direction of the McCann place. I thought that maybe we could explore some of the smaller country roads or the well-worn deer paths. Maybe Brandon had set off away from the winery and then just gotten farther than he had intended.

Once we were out of Plattsburgh on Boone's Passage, I nudged Rainy Day into a canter. He seemed to enjoy the speed, so I allowed him to break into a gallop on the straightaway. I had only let him gallop a couple of times before—Marty said you had to be a really experienced rider to let a horse flirt with the flight instinct—but I felt confident in Rainy Day's good sense. We would only gallop a mile or so, I told myself. And after all, we were in a hurry.

Not too far out of town, the road was blocked by a sheriff's car turned sideways. I slowed Rainy Day to a canter, then to a trot, then to a walk. We approached slowly. A couple of men in uniforms were standing around the car. I could hear muddled voices and static crackling from the dirty black two-way radio one of the men had hitched to his pants.

"I remember you," one of the deputies said, grinning. "The kid who saved that vet during the flash flood."

I leaned forward in the saddle and patted Rainy Day on his sweaty neck. "Well, my horse helped," I said.

"Yeah," one of the men said. "We were working up by the bridge where debris was jamming up. You were riding this guy."

"So you guys are blocking the road?"

"Yeah, county commissioner's son is missing. Eight-year-old kid. You haven't seen anything funny, have you? This kid's old lady's pretty frantic."

"I can believe it," I said. "Actually, I think he probably just wandered off someplace and got lost. I was with him a couple of hours ago, and he was just a plain old bored kid."

I told the deputies the story of the wedding preparations at Marie's Winery, how Brandon was parked on the porch in all the commotion.

"Anyway," I said, "can I get by? If I see anything I can always come back. It can't hurt."

"'Fraid not, young lady. We can't let anyone through," one of the deputies said. "Anyone includes you."

The deputies were friendly but adamant. I turned around and walked back in the direction of town. Around a bend in the road I brought Rainy Day to a halt.

"Forget this," I said, digging my right knee into his side and bringing the reins to the left gently. "This is what's called a U-turn, Rainy Day. There may be a roadblock, but who says we have to stay on the road?"

After a little bushwhacking, with dry branches snapping at my head left and right, Rainy Day and I managed to find a deer path in the direction I wanted to go. Soon there were more cedars and junipers than leafy trees, and the ground was covered with brown needles, cones, and puffballs. Eventually the path turned beaten down, as if someone had come through with a four-wheeler. There were fewer overhead branches brushing my head and raining ticks on me.

The deeper I looked into the woods, the more sure I was that someone had been cutting down trees. Stumps poked up in between the fully-grown cedars. "No Trespassing" signs were posted on the larger trunks, and "No Hunting" signs on others. Rainy Day stepped carefully and slowly, his hindquarters rolling side to side like a ship as he advanced. He blew air out of his lips and his ears twitched at every twig snap. I had no firm idea of where we were going, other than that I wanted to get past the roadblock and see if I could get out to the winery. The sun slanting through the trees gave me my bearings as I tried to envision our way back to the road.

Rainy Day was straining against the reins, wanting to go more quickly.

"Okay, boy," I said, giving him a little more freedom. "Let's see what you've got planned here."

Farther ahead we turned off the road onto a hayfield, went up and down a hill, crossed a dry creek, and came down another long hill. At the bottom, the woods opened up into a floodplain, and I realized that just ahead was the Missouri River itself. Calculating the distances and the layout of the area, I judged us to be about a mile downstream of the winery.

I heeled Rainy Day into a quick trot and saw the silvery brown water ahead. On the other side of the river, high gray bluffs of rock stood tall in the sunshine. We came to a stop on the levee and while Rainy Day caught his breath and stamped his hooves in the caked mud, I surveyed up and down the river. Was it my imagination, or did I really see something about a half mile farther downstream on the opposite shore? I shaded my eyes to cut down the glare and get a better view. Wedged into an eddy along the river's edge, trapped between a fallen tree and a large boulder, was a rowboat. I could see a small arm waving at me and a thin, high voice calling out. Just a little farther downstream was a two-lane bridge built in the 1950s. Big white waves churned around the bridge's pylons.

"No way!" I said aloud to Rainy Day. "Could that be Brandon Follette?" I knew I could never get across the river. I also knew that Brandon was in more danger than he realized. If he fell overboard, the swirling current that held his boat in place would drag him under and pin him there. If his boat got dislodged, it would continue drifting downstream and might slam into the bridge pylons. A wave of dread went from my head to my feet as I thought through my options.

"I hate to leave, but we've got to get help," I said quietly. Then I raised my voice and yelled to Brandon, "Stay there and don't move." I doubted he heard me, but at least he knew that I had seen him.

I turned Rainy Day, and we set off at a gallop back the way we came. Before getting to the road, though, Rainy

Day turned off in a new direction. After a few minutes of hard riding, we arrived at the northernmost boundary of the McCann farm. Without pausing, Rainy Day kept on trotting until we were at the hitching rail just outside the barn. He whinnied at Hannah and from inside the barn she returned the greeting.

I leaped off his back, threw the reins over the post, and ran toward the house.

Nelson was on the phone as I approached the front porch gasping for breath. He hung up and raised his eyebrows in surprise.

"Where'd you come from? I've been sitting here for the last hour. They've shut down Boone's Passage, and I was going to call you to say I'd take care of everything on my own this evening, not to bother coming. How'd the setup go? I haven't heard from Patti all day, not since Thursday, as a matter of fact. I don't even know why the road's closed. Was there an accident?"

"No accident," I said, huffing. "Well, yes, there was. We've got to get in the car and help, Nelson. Barbara Follette's son is missing and I think I just saw him in a rowboat out on the Missouri. He's trapped in an eddy. He must have gotten in the boat and untied it from the dock where the reception is going to be."

"You have got to be kidding," Nelson said in disbelief, checking to make sure he had car keys in his pocket. He stood up.

"I'm not. Let's go. We've got to go right now," I said.

Just then Buster got up from under Nelson's legs and began to wag his tail and bark. He ran out to the mailbox at the edge of the road and looked up the road. I heard the unmistakable sound of a horse-and-buggy coming in our direction. The glossy, energetic gelding pulled up to the mailbox before Mr. Rhinestat brought him to a halt. Sitting on the driver's seat next to Mr. Rhinestat was Esther. And next to Esther, beaming from ear to ear, was Brandon Follette.

"Brandon!" I practically screamed, dashing out toward the buggy. "I can't believe it. The whole county has been looking for you."

Brandon stopped smiling and looked down.

Mr. Rhinestat tipped his straw hat back on his head. "Seems this boy decided to go for a boat ride," he said. "Esther and I were just on our way back from paying a call and there he was under the bridge, just like the troll who tried to stop the Three Billy Goats Gruff. He's lucky we happened by."

Esther looked up at her father's face to check whether he was angry or kidding. When he smiled down at her, she wasn't the only one who was relieved. Brandon took the moment to start blurting his story.

"I didn't mean to go so far," he said. "I walked down to the dock, saw the boat there, and got in. For a while I just sat on a life jacket and read the comic book you gave me, but then I got bored again. So I slipped the rope off the pole. At first it was fun. Actually, the whole time it was fun. Did you see me stuck behind that rock?" Brandon asked me.

"Yeah," I said, deciding it was not worth telling him what might have happened if things had gone wrong.

"Well, after you left, the current got the boat loose, and the next thing I knew I was washed up under the bridge. That's when I saw him." Brandon pointed at Mr. Rhinestat, and we all turned to hear what happened.

"As I said," Mr. Rhinestat explained, "I just saw this little tyke all wedged up between the bridge support and the riverbank. I parked the buggy and climbed on down. I thought at first he was fishing. 'You picked an awful dangerous place to fish, son,' I said. Then I reached out over the boat and dragged him ashore. The boat's still there, but won't be for long if the current gets ahold of it."

"Hang on," Nelson said. "We've got to tell everyone you're okay. Brandon, what's your home phone?"

Brandon told him and jumped off the seat clear of the big iron buggy wheel. He went to the head of the docile, well-mannered buggy horse and patted his nose and face.

"Brandon, come here," Nelson said. "Your mom wants to talk to you."

Brandon ran to the porch and started talking a mile a minute. He hung up and said Mrs. Follette would be over in fifteen minutes to pick him up.

"What about the wedding?" I asked.

"She says it will start late. That will give my sister more time to put on her makeup," Brandon joked. He looked at Mr. Rhinestat. "She asked if you and Esther could wait 'til she gets here so she can thank you."

Mr. Rhinestat joined Nelson on the porch, and Brandon went off with Esther to check out the barn. Nelson asked me to stick with them just in case they wandered too far.

I showed Esther and Brandon old Moses. Brandon looked a little scared of the big hog whose blotchy gray-and-pink skin was caked with smelly dirt. Esther hopped right up onto the rail of his pen and admired his size and look.

"Can we give him something to eat?" she said.

"Sure," I said, and I passed her his slop bucket. She poured the brown goopy contents into his trough. With many grunts and snorts, old Moses heaved himself off his side and came over to eat, his tail snapping back and forth.

"Cool," Brandon said.

Everything in the barn went the same way—Brandon freaked out, Esther did something, then Brandon said "cool."

And then we heard a car pull into the driveway.

I wouldn't go so far as to say that Mrs. Follette was like

a different person, but she was definitely more humble. She hugged Brandon for a really long time and afterward wiped the tears from her eyes with a cotton hanky.

As soon as she was capable of looking away from Brandon, Nelson introduced her to Mr. Rhinestat, who had his arm around Esther.

"This is who brought your son back," Nelson said. "Actually, I think you may have met him once or twice at council meetings."

He looked at her meaningfully. "We never met in person," he said. "I was usually in a group."

Mrs. Follette shook his hand. "Thank you very much, Mr. Rhinestat. Our whole family is very grateful to you."

She stopped there. It was obviously hard for her to talk without crying. I looked at Nelson and wondered whether he might take this opportunity to bring up the buggy tax and cell tower problem. I couldn't imagine Mrs. Follette any more likely to cave in than now. He didn't say anything, though.

"Would you like something to drink, Mrs. Follette?" I offered. "A soda? Water?"

"Thank you, no," she said, blowing her nose one last time. "We really need to go back. It's nearly five-thirty and we have a wedding to pull off. Brandon and I have to dress." She put her arms around him again. "I guess I overreacted. My husband says I totally lost my head, but I was just so frightened. You hear about such terrible things happening."

As she and Brandon got in their car to leave, I couldn't resist making one last connection.

"You know, my aunt did the flowers for your daughter's wedding," I said.

"Patti? At Room for Blooms?" Mrs. Follette seemed genuinely surprised.

"Yes."

"Oh, well, everything is beautiful, just beautiful. I will be sure to tell her I saw you here, and what a help you've been. Now, I am sorry to dash, but as you can imagine, we have a church full of family and friends waiting for us. Come on, Brandon. Say thank you to Mr. Rhinestat and Mr. McCann."

"Thank you, Mr. Rhinestat. Thank you, Mr. McCann. Oh, wait a second, Mom."

Brandon ran to the buggy and climbed up into the black passenger section behind the driver's bench. The buggy rocked a little on its large wheels while he was out of sight. Then he came back down holding the book I had given him and offered it to me.

I laughed. "You can keep that, Brandon. It was a gift."

"Really? Thanks," he said, and then they drove off.

"Can you sit a minute?" Nelson asked Mr. Rhinestat. "I've found a couple of interesting precedents that we can use when making our case. Both cases, I should say. And I'd love to go over them with you."

Esther's eyes gleamed at me, as if to say how much she hoped her father would say yes so that she and I could play.

"I trust what you say," Mr. Rhinestat said. "But Esther and I must go on home. We've been gone all day and have chores to do. Her mother will be wondering where we are."

Esther hung her head as they walked over to the buggy. Esther climbed onto the driver's bench and Mr. Rhinestat unclipped the reins from the fence and passed them over the back of his horse into Esther's hands. After he mounted, he looked over to us.

"You have a nice place here, Mr. McCann," he said. "Now you just need a family to help you take care of it." I was shocked to see Mr. Rhinestat wink. Before Nelson could respond, Mr. Rhinestat continued.

"There's a barn raising on Wednesday over at the Shoemachers'. They're outside of Prescott, the next town over, and we expect a hundred people will show up. Families driving from all over, helping out, spending the night. I'd be pleased if you and April here might want to come over to see how it's done."

"I'll have to check with April's aunt, but we'd be honored, Mr. Rhinestat, thank you," Nelson said.

Mr. Rhinestat backed up the buggy and shook the reins onto the horse's back gently. "Just drive into Prescott and ask for the Shoemacher place," he said. "You can't miss it. Look for a barn with fifty men crawling all over the roof. That will be us."

The horse trotted away at a brisk clip and in a minute the buggy was out of sight.

"What's a barn raising?" I asked after Nelson and I had returned to the porch and sat down in our usual places.

"Just what it sounds like," he said. "A few dozen families get together on a workday and build a barn in one day. The women and children make and serve the food, and the men and older boys construct the barn. I've only seen pictures of it. It'll be an experience, that's for sure."

chapter

That Wednesday I got an earlier start than usual and finished my chores at Nelson's as quickly as I could. When I found him in the kitchen afterward he was on the phone, deep in what seemed to be a serious conversation, so I wrote a long note saying I would meet him at the barn raising. I asked him to hitch the horse trailer to the truck in case I thought Rainy Day was just too tired to ride all the way back to Plattsburgh.

It was a beautiful ride. The road opened and passed up and down through green hills and rich-looking farm country. The farther we got from Plattsburgh, the less scrubby and wooded the landscape looked. Rainy Day and I arrived in the center of Prescott close to two o'clock. Prescott was a miniscule town, really just a crossroads of two streets—Main and First. Instead of traffic signals, there was only a four-way stop. I passed a bank, a tiny town hall, and a general store. One block away was a section of out-of-use train tracks. Next to the defunct train track's were three or four silos and some oversize grain machinery. It didn't look like any of these machines had been used in decades, but once upon a time they must have been the reason Prescott existed in the first place—to get grain and corn and other crops off the farms and into the cities. Beyond the silos, a steel water tank loomed high over the town on wooden supports. Faded letters spelled Prescott on the side of the tank. The town felt abandoned. It seemed like one of those places old Mr. McCann was talking about when he told history stories about our area. I half expected a rebel soldier to come limping along from the creek.

Just then an older woman came out of the post office. She had a big purse hanging from her arm and was walking to a rusty old car parked across the street. I urged Rainy Day forward and said, "Excuse me, I'm looking for the Shoemachers'?"

The woman had so much foundation on her face that she looked orange, especially compared to the pale cream shade of her bare arms. Her eyebrows were brown pencil lines and her short curly hair was a kind of bluish white. She smiled up at me and pointed to the road leading west out of town.

"Just a mile or two thataway," she said. "Can't miss it. Big white farmhouse on a hill to your right."

"Thank you," I called as I gave Rainy Day a nudge with my heels.

The first thing I noticed was the dozens of black buggies. They were all lined up near one of the farm buildings, their shafts resting down in the grass. Each one had an orange reflective triangle on the back and battery-operated lights so they could be seen at night. I guessed that all the horses had been turned out in the pasture somewhere.

"Hang out here for a while," I said to Rainy Day, switching his bridle for a halter so he would be more comfortable. I attached him to a long lead line so that he could graze below the fence where I fastened the other end. "If you're invited, I'll turn you out so you can go make some friends, too."

Rainy Day's eyes were bright and shining. He shook his head and I could tell he approved of this place.

The farm was large and well cared for. All the fences were in good repair, and well-cultivated fields of corn, soy, or oats rolled off in every direction. Near the freshly painted main house was a plot of kitchen crops like beets, carrots, lettuces, and other vegetables. I also recognized blackberry and blueberry bushes and strawberry plants. I took my time walking to the main house and noticed a small gas generator droning outside the kitchen window. Mr. Rhinestat had explained to me that many Amish families used generators to power appliances like refrigerators and fans, especially in the summer. The generator noise faded as I approached the scene of the barn raising, where I could hear voices singing behind a stand of large old pin oaks.

I found the half-built barn, still a skeleton of wood. Mr. Rhinestat wasn't joking when he said that by the time I got there there would be fifty men crawling all over the roof. Perched on the raw beams and crosspieces, each man wielded a hammer. They were dressed alike—the same straw hats, the same navy pants, and shirts either light blue, dark blue, or white. They leaned into their work, laying heavy pieces of wood and pounding nails. Down on the grass or standing on top of piles of lumber, other men passed the wood upward into the waiting hands of those who were in the rafters.

Women and children milled and worked around the site. The women's plain dresses reminded me of a bouquet of flowers—blue, pale green, light yellow, and lavender. The strings of their white bonnets dangled on their shoulders casually. Some of the women sat on piles of raw planks of tan wood. Others stood in small groups, their arms folded across their chests as they chatted and watched the men. A few lounged on the grass, their legs stretched out in front of them. I tried to find Mrs. Rhinestat but everyone blended into the scene. It was hard to tell one person from another.

Off to the east where the ground was level, a bunch of girls played with a long jump rope. A group of boys, barefoot and in long dark pants, was running around playing tag. Some other boys had a softball game going. The really little kids were sitting under a tree with some older girls.

"April!"

I turned and saw Esther running barefoot toward me from the far side of the house. She was holding the hand of another girl in a knee-length navy blue dress.

"We're just playing dolls over there and I saw you. This is Sarah."

"Hi, Sarah."

Sarah's eyes bulged as she said hi and I realized that to her I must look a little scary—or at least weird. I mean, I was obviously a girl but I was wearing long cargoes and a tank top. And my head was uncovered. If it had not been for Esther, I was sure Sarah would have never had the courage to say hi.

"This is amazing," I said to Esther.

"What?" she asked, puzzled.

"This. This whole scene." I waved my hand. To Esther

the barn raising was homey and familiar, while to me it was exotic, just another way our worlds were so very different.

"Do you want to come play with us?"

"Sure. I was thinking I'd say hi to your mom first. Where is she?"

Esther pointed into the field of pastel dresses at one corner of the unfinished barn.

"Right over there."

Around the back side of the barn site, I saw long tables pushed up next to one another. Covered casseroles sat in trays filled with ice, and old steel milk cans were being used as water coolers. They had already had their big lunch break and would now just keep going until the barn was completed. I hoped Nelson would get here before they were done so he could see the construction.

Mrs. Rhinestat greeted me with a friendly nod. "I am glad you could make it, April," Mrs. Rhinestat said, smiling. "Esther was hoping to see you, too."

"Yeah, I just saw her and her friend Sarah over there. She invited me to go play dolls with them."

"As you like," Mrs. Rhinestat said. "As you can see, we use these days to catch up on the news of our extended family and friends, some of whom we only see at barn raisings."

She didn't introduce me to the women she was standing with, but we all smiled at one another and said, "Good day." I was growing more used to the reserve of the Amish. Their manner now struck me as more respectful than cold.

I turned and went back to where Esther and her friends were playing. They made a space for me in their circle and passed me a doll. It never occurred to them that I was too old to be playing with dolls, so I played along. A cheer went up from the softball game; someone had hit a grand slam. Within a minute or two I lost myself in the sounds of the scene—the shouts of encouragement and constant banging from the men on the barn, the murmur from the women at the base, the happy yells from the boys playing, and the singsong chants from the girls jumping. Glancing up, I noticed a jet cruising by high in the sky, the roar of its engines muffled by the distance. The plane was leaving a thin white streak across the expanse of blue, a reminder that some people in this world traveled faster than sound.

"Rainy Day!" I said aloud, remembering that I had meant to turn him out to graze. I excused myself and ran from the barn site, around the main house, and toward where I had left him.

I hadn't needed to worry. Rainy Day seemed to be having a conversation with two well-built buggy horses—

one black and one a rich dark brown—who had joined him where he was fastened to the fence. I patted him and gave him a kiss on the neck.

"It's nice here, isn't it?" I murmured. He swished his tail and rubbed his muzzle under my arm.

Just then Nelson and Aunt Patti pulled up in the pickup. I was relieved to see that he had remembered to attach the trailer. There was no way Rainy Day should go all the way back to Plattsburgh on foot. It was too far for me, too.

"Sorry we're so late," he said, climbing out of the driver's seat. "Working everything out took longer than I expected."

"Hey, babe," Aunt Patti said, taking my hand.

I smiled. "Nelson, what do you mean, 'working everything out'?"

"You'll see." He looked over at Rainy Day. "He sure seems happy."

"This is horse heaven," I said. "Come on. You're not going to believe this."

Nelson whistled when he saw the simple barn structure taking shape under the tens of figures hammering all over and inside it.

"It reminds me of an anthill or a beehive," he said. "But

also completely human. You can't believe all this can happen in one day, but then you realize the power of lots of people all working with a single goal. Tomorrow at this time, this family will have a whole new beautiful barn."

Mr. Rhinestat and Ammann were drinking cold apple cider and talking with a group of men when Nelson and I approached. Aunt Patti had wandered over to Mrs. Rhinestat to introduce herself.

"Glad you could make it," Mr. Rhinestat said, looking at me. "My wife told me you were over with Esther and the girls."

"This is an amazing sight," Nelson said, a big wave of his arm including everything.

"It gets the job done," Mr. Rhinestat said.

"And then some," Nelson said. "Anyway, I have some good news for you, Mr. Rhinestat."

"Yes?"

"I've spent much of the last few days negotiating with Harold Bloom, the chief attorney for the county. I pointed out to him several instances where the community as a whole has absorbed the extra cost of maintaining a public property—signage and ramps for handicapped citizens, for example, but there are many other examples—technically incurred by a minority. The long and the short of it is that

Bloom agreed just this morning that the proposed buggy tax is illegal and discriminatory. It's a dead letter. And Mrs. Follette has agreed to drop the matter completely."

"I am glad to hear it," he said. "You have been kind to take this on, Mr. McCann. I am sure that the Old Order families around Plattsburgh would like to pay you for your services."

"And I am sure I will accept nothing but your gracious words," Nelson said. "It was the right thing to do. It's done, and that's all that matters. And as for the other matter—"

"The telephone tower?"

"Yes. That's taken care of as well."

"How so?"

"None of your concern, Mr. Rhinestat. I think all parties are satisfied, and that's enough for me and should be enough for you, seeing as how we're practically neighbors."

I had never heard Nelson sound so assured and official before. Of course I wondered how he had gotten that cell tower thing all figured out, but the timing didn't seem right to ask.

Mr. Rhinestat took Nelson's right hand in both of his and shook it warmly. "Well, I guess me and Ammann here had better get back on that roof. Ready, son?"

He clapped Ammann on the shoulder and they turned away. Another moment, and they had climbed back into the swarm of straw hats, suspenders, and homemade shirts. The sound of hammers on nails rang in the air.

chapter

Around five-thirty the barn raising was still in high gear but Nelson and I were ready to leave. The women were setting up a late afternoon meal—sandwiches and fruit—that the men and boys would come down and eat in shifts. Before they all broke for supper, I said good-bye to Esther and the girls and went over to drag Aunt Patti away. She seemed perfectly happy chatting with the women about various methods of preserving fruits. I led her back to Nelson, who asked one of the white-bearded old men he had been talking to to pass his good-bye along to Mr. Rhinestat.

I walked Rainy Day into the trailer and climbed into the front seat, where I ended up squashed between Nelson and Aunt Patti. As Nelson pulled slowly out of the parking area, I saw Ammann standing on a picnic bench, waving good-bye.

If I were Amish, I thought, I would be all done with school on my fourteenth birthday, now less than a month away. Like Ammann, I would be free to do real work on the farm. Then again, if I were Amish I could only do about half of what I liked to do—the girl's half, which included cooking, cleaning, and taking care of smaller children and babies. Then I would grow up and do the woman's half, which included more cooking, more cleaning, and more taking care of children and babies. I knew that wouldn't be my own path in life, but at the same time the barn raising had definitely changed the way I thought about people like the Rhinestats. They were different from me, but for the first time ever, I stopped thinking that "different" automatically meant "worse." It wasn't like they chained one another to the community. They really did choose to follow their traditions—at least once they were grown up. And the kids—at least the younger ones—seemed perfectly happy. Happier than most of the kids I knew. Something about the way they lived was working.

We pulled into our driveway close to seven o'clock. Nelson and Aunt Patti went straight into the house but I took my time getting Rainy Day settled and fed.

"What a day," I said, hanging all the tack up on its proper hooks and banging the dust out of the saddle blanket.

I took the currycomb and brush and, while Rainy Day

munched on his feed I gave him a thorough grooming. "Tomorrow you'll get a bath, I promise. Did you like meeting all those buggy horses? Was it hard to leave?"

Rainy Day threw his head up and curled his lips, blowing out a blast of air. Then he turned to look at me while he chewed.

"I guess it was," I said, cupping his chin in my hand and looking into his eye. I wondered how I would manage caring for him during the school year. It had been the best summer of my life. The thought of trading the farm routine for the school routine made me depressed. I worried that my brain just wouldn't be able to make the switch back to homework, tests, and papers, not to mention all the social stuff everyone had to deal with. I would be in eighth grade, when we were supposed to be middle-school leaders who would set good examples for the younger kids at all times. And what about summer reading? I still hadn't read more than five pages of *Into Thin Air*, and I would be expected to talk about it on the first day. Probably write something, too.

And what about JP? How would I be able to keep up with the foal's training? What if he ended up with a million bad habits because I couldn't spend enough time working with him? Would Marty be able to pitch in if I asked him to?

The sun was going down earlier as August rolled toward September, and by the time I came into the house it was nearly dark out. Nelson was helping Aunt Patti make dinner and music was blasting from the living room—early-nineties stuff that Lowell constantly made fun of. The wedding behind her, Aunt Patti had finally relaxed. It also helped that Mrs. Follette had made a special point to compliment her work and pass her an envelope with a huge cash tip. Now the only thing she had to complain about were the two dozen watermelons in her fridge at the shop, and one big fat one taking up the whole bottom shelf of our fridge in the house.

"April, why don't you go see if Lowell wants to come over for supper? I see his light on but I know his folks aren't home yet."

I was too lazy to walk all the fifteen steps to his back door, so I just yelled toward his open window for him to come over.

"Well, I could have done that," she said, playfully snapping a dish towel in my direction.

Over dinner Nelson and I talked about the barn raising, and Lowell said he wished he could have been there to see it for himself.

"The thing is," Nelson said, "they really are a living window into the old ways and customs."

"Only they live in the here and now," I said, trying to figure out exactly what seemed so exotic about the Amish. "They live as if nothing has changed, or in spite of things having changed. It's hard to explain. When I'm with them, I always feel a little left out, especially because I know they've chosen a way of life that leaves people like us out on purpose."

"It's complicated," Nelson said. "And it's tempting to turn them into a lesson. A history lesson. Or a lesson in ethics. Or in prudence or piety. But they're really just people and they don't want to be a living lesson. That's my sense anyway. It explains why they're so guarded."

"I guess they have to be guarded," Lowell said, sounding more mature than I often gave him credit for. "As soon as you let stuff in—TVs, air conditioners, cars—the best of the old days starts to go. The big mistake people make is to resist change. You gotta go with the flow."

Aunt Patti looked at him with a smile of approval. "I'm just glad everything worked out with that tax and the cell phone situation," she said, scraping all the rest of the sliced tomato salad onto Lowell's plate.

"Oh, right," I said. "I knew there was something else I meant to ask. How *did* you work out that cell phone tower thing?"

"Oh, that." Nelson didn't look up from his plate. He appeared to be very busy trimming the skin off his chicken. "I just found another site for the tower. It's almost as good, and not on Amish land. BeneTran was willing to accept a compromise site if the alternative was being shut out of the county altogether."

"Oh, yeah, where?" Aunt Patti said, interested.

"Oh, just this ridge at the southernmost corner of Pop's place. Although I suppose I should start calling it *my* place." He looked up at each of us in turn.

"Huh?" I was trying to understand.

"It's heavily wooded, so the tower won't be obtrusive. It's only thirty-five-feet tall, and they can make it look like a tree trunk so you'd hardly notice it."

"A cell phone tower disguised as a tree," Aunt Patti said, kind of disgusted.

"Well, that's more attractive than a tree disguised as a cell phone tower," Lowell said.

Nelson laughed. "Truth is," he said, "it *is* better for this part of the state to be networked this way."

"But what about your prospective buyer?" Aunt Patti said. "How do you know they'll be okay with a cell phone tower on the land, even an unobtrusive one?"

"Well . . ." Nelson wiped his mouth with his napkin.

"I've decided to stay. I've given notice with the public defender's office and I'm going to relocate here. I'll take some clients, but mainly I'll be looking after the farm. It dawned on me that this is where I belong."

Nelson was looking straight into Aunt Patti's eyes. She said nothing for a second, then looked down and took off her glasses and rubbed her nose. Then she reached out across the table to squeeze his hand. For Lowell and me, it was an awkward moment. Thank goodness Lowell decided the time was right to lean under the table to feed Chase a piece of chicken.

Nelson broke the silence he created.

"So I guess our friend Barbara Follette can thank us for two things: helping find her son and enriching her holdings as a shareholder in BeneTran. Who'd have thought it?"

Aunt Patti smiled at Nelson. No, she more than smiled. She downright glowed at him. Lowell kicked me hard under the table, as if I didn't notice where things seemed to be heading.

Oh, well, I thought, getting up to clear the table and serve dessert, considering all the changes in the air, *sometimes all a person can do is eat watermelon.*

Glossary

bay—a reddish brown color used to describe horses

bridle—the entire headpiece, including the bit, chinstrap, reins, and headstall

canter—one of a horse's four basic gaits, a three-beat gait

colt—a male horse under four years old that has not been castrated

croup—the rump, or back part, of a horse

currycomb—a plastic or rubber comb with several rows of short flexible bristles used for grooming

dam—a horse's mother

dock—the solid part of the animal's tail, not the hair

farrier—a person who shoes horses, a blacksmith

fetlock—the tufted, cushionlike projection on the back side of the leg above the horse's hoof

filly—a young female horse less than three or four years old

foal—a male or female horse less than one year old and still drinking its mother's milk

gallop—the fastest gait a horse can run

gelding—a male horse who cannot reproduce (unlike a stallion)

girth—a band or strap around the body of a horse that secures the saddle

halter—a harness of leather or rope that fits over a horse's head and is used for leading a horse

hock—the joint in the horse's hind legs similar to the human ankle

hoof pick—a metal or strong plastic tool with a pointed end for picking debris out of the underside of the hooves

hot-blooded—a horse whose ancestry can be traced back to the Arabian, Barb, Turk, or Thoroughbred; hot-bloods are intelligent, athletic, spirited, and competitive by nature, and can be temperamental and challenging to keep

mare—a female horse over four years old

Morgan—the oldest breed of horse originating in the United States, descended from a strong, fast, gentle, intelligient, and patient horse belonging to a Vermont schoolmaster named Justin Morgan in 1789

nicker—a sound a horse makes, presumably to communicate a greeting

paddock—an outdoor enclosure where horses are turned out for grazing

pastern—part of the leg between the hoof and the fetlock

pinto—a pattern of horse coloring characterized by two colors in particular patterns

poll—the topmost part of the head of the horse rear—to rise up onto the hind legs

roan—a horse hair color characterized by a gray or white thickly interspersed with other colors such as bay, chestnut, brown, or gray

stallion—a male horse who can reproduce (unlike a gelding)

stifle—the joint in the horse's leg similar to a human knee

tack—all gear and equipment that can be worn by a horse, including the bridle, saddle, bit, and halter

Thoroughbred—a breed of horse used as a racehorse and for hunting and jumping

trot—a two-beat gait, with the legs moving together diagonally

walk—one of the four basic gaits, a four-beat movement where each leg move independently and each hoof strikes the ground separately

withers—the slight ridge on the back of the horse

whinny—a low neighing sound